AS FLOWERS GO

Escape to Homeland Amazonia

ILKO MINEV

This book is in loving honor of muy parents, Mincho and Eva, my uncle Licco and Aunt Berta, my dear grandmother "Babushka" and also of the dearly departed Samuel Benchimol, who introduced me to the mysteries of the Amazon.
I miss them all very much.

ACKNOWLEDGMENTS

Many people contributed to this book. First and foremost, I would like to express my gratitude to Nora, my wife, best friend, and first reader, my children, Denis and Ilana, and my grandsons, Samuel and Eli. My brother, Slavko, and my cousins Salvator and Max were also of great help in reconstructing the saga of our family, which was the inspiration behind this story, a blend of many true facts with a bit of fiction. Without their enthusiastic collaboration and encouragement, none of this would have been possible. In this account, all character names are fictional, with the exception of public figures.

Lastly, I would like to extend a special thanks to Lilian Álvares and Professor José Rincón.

CONTENTS

CHAPTER I

The World As I Saw It

In the autumn of my life, before illness or senility silence me, I feel the need to share the memories and lessons I've accumulated over the course of 90 years. It took me quite a while to convince myself that it was important to set down these recollections, exhortations, and recommendations for my children, grandchildren, great-grandchildren, and anyone else who might want to learn a bit more about these events from the past. I hope that when they read this one day they'll remember me fondly and with pride and gratitude. And I know Berta would stand wholeheartedly behind my decision.

I'm in a hurry. I'm afraid something unforeseen may keep me from completing my task. My health has been failing in recent years. I'm no longer the strong, independent person I once was. I'm so much less mobile than I used to be. Until a short time ago, I had no trouble driving, but now my car sits useless in the garage, rusting away. I'm not comfortable behind the wheel, but I don't want to hire a driver either. Fortunately, there's always someone around to help out when I need it, and my family is always paying me visits. I'm very grateful, especially to my grandchildren and great-grandchildren, who could easily find more entertaining things to occupy their time.

I've always liked to travel, but lately because it's so hard for me to get around, I don't enjoy it as much and I'd just as soon stay home. I thank God I'm still lucid and my sight is good. My memory works perfectly, and I don't think I'm a heavy burden for my family yet. I read quite a lot and watch television. So my life still has some meaning. I've turned down every single invitation to live with my daughter Sara or my son, Daniel. I know these invitations have been sincere, but I'd be unhappy and I'd lose some of my independence. I enjoy a solid position financially, thanks to my savings and to the skyrocketing appreciation of real estate values in recent years, so I don't require any monetary assistance. I'm not a wealthy man, but I can afford a comfortable life. At my age, this is a blessing.

My children have always been understanding, and they leave me to my own devices here in our longtime family home, where my housekeeper, Terezinha, lives too. She's been with me for more than 30 years, going back to when Berta was still alive. Terezinha is an expert when it comes to taking care of me and of the house too. It's just the two of us, plus Quilate, my German shepherd. Though he's old, like me, he's still my best friend and protector. You wouldn't think he was a dog. He sleeps on the terrace, next to my room – and pity the poor fool who ventures to enter without an invitation.

A few months ago, things took a turn for the better: Rebeca, my youngest, decided to come to live with me while she attends college. My days are happier with her around. Like her mother 20 years ago, Rebeca provides me with tender loving care, especially on the long rainy days of the hot Amazonian winter.

I have hardly any neighbors. One by one, the houses in downtown Manaus have turned into businesses. Because these shops and office buildings are so close by, my home serves as a parking lot for the whole family when they're in the area, and I end up with more visitors. On these occasions, we chat and talk about the latest news, and I tell my endless stories until I'm worn out. I often find myself frustrated, because young people know so little about the past. It seems they don't even remember historical facts from just a few years back. Not long ago, I could have talked this over with my friends. But one by one, they've gone. I miss them terribly, and they've left a huge void. I lost my chess partner quite recently. Ironically enough, the latest one to succumb was my doctor – and he was nearly 20 years younger than I am.

In short, I'm in a hurry, because at my age, I know there's not much time left. And I'm well aware that as the years go by, my memories will fade, and the world will make serious or petty mistakes and get up to its old tricks again, like a merry-go-round that never stops. I've lived through rough and turbulent times. It's been proven throughout history that ordinary folks pay a high price for the errors and omissions of the past. I was lucky. I survived. Many others didn't. It is in their memory – and especially in remembrance of my friend Salvator, whom I miss so very much – that I feel the obligation to bear witness to this story. I hope my descendants will read about my past and remember it, learn from it, and take pride in it. I want this to make it easier for them to cope wisely, eagerly, and responsibly with whatever challenges might come their way.

As best I can, I want to relay the events that I witnessed before, during, and after the Second World War. Perhaps this will help ensure that those long, dreadful years will never be forgotten and that the pain and suffering will not have been in vain. It's time we learned from the lessons of the past and kept ideology, economics, and racial, ethnic, and religious issues, or anything else, from serving as justification for dictatorships, concentration camps, holocausts, torture, and other crimes against humanity. Tragically, history shows that there have always been people willing to commit these crimes -and there is no dearth of them now. For this reason, certain lessons of the past will always maintain relevance.

I'm also going to relay the part of recent Amazonian history with which I'm very familiar. I want to tell you about the place that took me in when I fled the slaughter in Europe, the place that became my home and my passion. The Amazon is still writing its history today, as areas of its immense demographic void are being occupied at an ever-faster pace and the agricultural frontier advances. I'm not a historian, sociologist, or anthropologist, and I have no great pretensions. I'm simply going to recount my life since March 4, 1944, the day I arrived in Belém, the gateway of the Amazon, carried here by fate and by pure chance. I have a sharp memory of my first sensation: I felt I had landed on another planet, so great was the difference between the world I'd come from and the new one I was just beginning to know. I couldn't imagine that I'd live here for the rest of my life and that I'd fall in love with the place, a place where I would face challenges of a totally unprecedented nature.

But my tale truly begins 24 years earlier in Sofia, Bulgaria. Here is my story.

CHAPTER II

Bulgaria

I was born on March 5, 1920, in Sofia, the capital of Bulgaria. My young parents, Rebeca and Daniel Hazan, decided to name me, their first-born son, Licco, in honor of my great-grandfather. My first memories are from 1925, when a huge explosion blew *Sveta Nedelya Cathedral* to smithereens, right in the heart of downtown Sofia. It was an act of terrorism, an attempt to kill Tsar Boris III, but he got lucky: He was in transit and escaped unscathed. We lived close to the main square, and we watched people covered in blood be hauled away to the hospital. It made such an impression on me that the resounding explosion and ensuing scene echoed in my nightmares for years. As so often the case with terrorist acts, many innocent people died. This violence contrasted with the provincial atmosphere of our small capital city.

The early 20th century wasn't the best era to begin your life in this part of the world. My brief childhood and youth weren't at all easy, nor was the history of my country. In 1878, after Bulgaria had freed itself from the Ottoman yoke with the decisive aid of Russia, the country entered a period of turbulence, provoked chiefly by deluded rulers who sought to re-establish the great and powerful nation that

Bulgaria had been 600 years earlier, before the Ottomans had defeated and enslaved it. Our new country was born when the treaties of San Stefano and Berlin were signed, both guaranteed by what were then the world powers, Russia, Austria-Hungary, Germany, France, and England, all engaged in a silent battle for influence over this corner of Europe. Because Bulgaria occupied the strategic central area of the Balkans, it played a crucial role in this dispute.

The struggle to control lands in East Macedonia and Thrace sparked a number of conflicts between Bulgaria, Greece, Serbia, Montenegro, and Turkey. Casting aside their discord in 1912, the four countries of the Balkan Peninsula joined forces against the Ottoman Empire with the clear ambition of conquering the Turks' last remaining dominions in Europe. The Balkan War broke out and Bulgaria was victorious – or at least until the division of the conquered territories.

In 1913, Serbia and Greece formed a new alliance, this time against Bulgaria. The Ottoman Empire eventually counter-attacked and even Romania ended up with part of our territory. We lost the war and had to face all the bitter consequences. Defeated, Bulgaria aligned itself with Germany and Austria-Hungary and in 1914 entered World War I, plainly intent on seeking revenge against its neighbors. When the country lost the Great War as well, King Ferdinand was forced to abdicate in favor of his son, Boris III. This series of losses obliged the country to cede the Aegean coast to Greece. We lost almost all of Macedonia to the new state of Yugoslavia and, on top of it, we had to give the Bulgarian bread basket, Dobrudzha, back to the Romanians. The country lay in ruins, while it also owed overwhelming reparations to neighboring nations and had to take in waves of refugee brothers from lost territories.

As if the two wars had not devastated Bulgaria enough, the world sank into a deep recession in 1929, prolonging the country's political chaos and economic disaster for more than a decade. A few years later, in 1939, World War II – the bloodiest conflict history has ever seen – broke out. Those hard years left deep marks on me. Although our politicians displayed imprudence and a lack of common sense, a sizable portion of the Bulgarian population learned a great deal from the suffering of that period. Our people became liberal and tolerant, embracing ethical values rarely seen in more developed nations. In retrospect, it's obvious that ordinary Bulgarian citizens had the good judgment and wisdom lacking in their leaders.

The country's population encompassed a variety of ethnic minorities – Turks, Jews, Armenians, and Gypsies – all living in relative peace and harmony with the Bulgarian majority. This ethnic diversity, along with a proximity to the Mediterranean Sea, accounts for Bulgaria's splendid cuisine, which features a panoply of lamb dishes, appetizingly rich salads, and delectable cheeses and yogurts. Moreover, it is the land of exclusive wines pressed from rare grapes that are native to the region and date back to the ancient civilization of the Thracians.

Fully restored after the 1925 attack, a magnificent Eastern Orthodox church, Sveta Nedelya, still stands in Sofia's main square, just a two-minute walk from a mosque. Another two minutes beyond that is a large and lovely synagogue, which has long been the biggest *Sephardic* temple in Europe. In all my many years, I've never known another European city with so much religious diversity and tolerance.

Financial troubles forced me to leave school and start working early. I was a Jewish boy raised by his grandfather. I lost my mother when I was 2); she died whilegiving birth to my only brother, David. My father passed away nine years later, in 1932. He died unexpectedly, probably from a heart attack, after he had gone bankrupt and lost everything in the recession then plaguing the world. He had grown bitter, never having gotten over his wife's sudden death. Losing the business that supported his children was too much for that kind man. I hold him very dear to my heart.

I quit studying at the German school, one of the best in the city, not long after my *bar mitzvah*, where I had read lengthy stretches of the *Torah* in Ancient Hebrew – and fluently at that. This is the confirmation and coming-of-age ceremony celebrated in the Jewish religion when a boy turns 13 and is initiated into community life. At that tender age, I went to work as a shop boy and apprentice mechanic at an auto garage owned by an acquaintance of my grandfather.

The fact that I had learned *Ladino* at home, the language of Sephardic Jews, was a great advantage for me. The Jews who were expelled from the Iberian Peninsula by the Inquisition in the late 15th century preserved this old form of Spanish, which dates to the time of Cervantes. It later proved extremely useful, given its remarkable similarity to the Portuguese language spoken in Brazil.

The German language stayed with me from school, along with the habit of reading, a sense of responsibility and punctuality, and some general knowledge that would later come in handy in life. In the early half of the 20th century, speaking fluent German was vital. German culture was highly valued in Bulgaria then, esteemed and disseminated by a significant slice of the elite. Both politically and culturally and in terms of popular tastes as well, the country was in fact divided between Russophiles and Germanophiles. Alongside the enthusiasts of German culture, part of the people admired Russia, the country that had broken the chains of the 500-year-long Ottoman oppression. Moreover, the Russians used the same Cyrillic alphabet and were Slavs, like the Bulgarian majority. While they are wholly distinct languages, Bulgarian and Russian have many similarities. Both countries' Eastern Orthodox religions are quite similar as well. You could find signs of gratitude, friendship, and admiration for Russia everywhere.

This was the setting in Bulgaria, and these were the political forces: on the one hand, the fascist Germanophile government and, on the other, Russian sympathizers. On the eve of the great conflict that erupted in 1939, we, young Bulgarians, didn't realize a world catastrophe was heading toward us at the speed of a runaway train.

When I was young, in the latter half of the 1930s, I liked to enjoy the Bulgarian countryside in the summer and go for long treks in the mountains around Sofia. In the winter, I'd go skiing. On these outings, a good share of my friends and companions were Eastern Orthodox Bulgarians, and we couldn't have gotten along better. Fewer than 50,000 Jews lived in Bulgaria, or less than 1 percent of the total population. People generally treated us well, and we were readily accepted by most. For all intents and purposes, we felt like Bulgarians. We loved the country and took pride in its millennial culture. True, there was some anti-Semitism, but it was not manifested in the same way or intensity as in other European countries.

After nearly two years as an apprentice, I turned into a fine mechanic, sought after by wealthy car owners. I managed to earn enough to keep my brother in school and help my grandfather pay the expenses of our modest household. I was proud of myself and confident in the future.

At the time my father passed away, my grandfather Elia had been in poor health for some time, due to the years

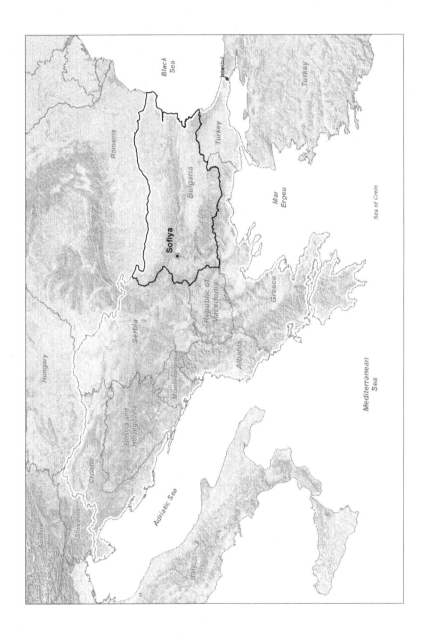

he'd spent in the trenches during the Balkan War and World War I. In my earliest memories of him, my grandfather walked with a limp and complained about his horrendously painful rheumatism, especially in the winter. To our good fortune, he had inherited a nice apartment and a well-situated shop from our great-grandparents. Our grandmother was from an affluent family and had also bequeathed us some valuable jewelry. Shortly before my grandfather died, he sold the jewelry and the store and paid off a good share of my father's debts. There was even some money left over, and that helped support us a while.

My grandfather hadn't worked for some time due to his war injuries. On the other hand, because he was well respected, religious, and highly educated, he was quite popular in artistic circles and was friends with many writers and journalists. I have a clear memory of how indignant he was about the persecutions that came in retaliation for the attack on Tsar Boris. The government used this act of violence as a pretext for getting rid of a number of intellectuals who were critical of the regime, including some of my grandfather's acquaintances. Famous writers like Joseph (Jossif) Herbst and Geo Milev, among many others, simply disappeared while in the custody of policemen hell-bent on vengeance. I can now recognize this as a foreshadowing of the inhumanities that would be committed by the Bulgarian fascists in the years to come.

Since my grandfather knew how to pray fluently and had a wonderful voice, he managed to supplement his income as a *chazan*, or cantor, at the synagogue. He said the art of singing had been a family tradition for 500 years, starting in the city of Toledo, and that our name derived from this talent. Not even the protracted illness and subsequent death of my grandfather in 1938 – may his memory be a blessing – shook my confidence in the future. I was 18 by then and my brother, David, 16. We were mature enough to handle life, we had inherited a comfortable home from our grandfather, and, although we had no family nearby, our friends, neighbors, and more distant relatives showered us with affection.

* * * * *

Everything got even better when a tall, thin, and well-dressed elderly gentleman pulled into our shop in a big fancy car one day. I'd seen him on occasion at synagogue and on the Jewish high holidays. People knew him as a rich man who had made substantial money in the tobacco trade. I'd also heard he was a good, just man and that while he wasn't very religious, he aided the poor, treated his employees well, and always contributed to community causes. He was from the Farhi family, but I didn't know his first name. I waited for him to approach me, figuring he was there to have his car repaired. He greeted me and went straight to the subject.

"My name is Leon Farhi, and I'm the new owner of this business."

We were all quiet, not knowing what to say. It was a small team, made up of another mechanic and a shop boy. Our boss, the garage owner – my late grandfather's friend – had been sick for months. He had tuberculosis, and word was that he'd reached the terminal stage of the disease. In a way, it was not surprising that the garage had been sold, yet we stood in nervous silence as the new owner looked over the small premises. Much to everyone's relief, he continued the conversation with these words: "This garage is now part of the American Car Company, and, if you want, you are its newest employees." Though we were still reeling from the news, we breathed a sigh of relief.

"As you probably know, the American Car Company

represents General Motors and its European division, Opel, in Bulgaria," he went on. We certainly did know it. What we hadn't known was that Mr. Farhi had his hand in this business as well. We had actually done some work for the American Car Company, which wasn't far from our garage. It was the best in the business in Sofia, and I felt like we'd won the lottery that day. Not only had we kept our jobs; we were now employees of a solid company with an excellent reputation.

"Mr. Licco Hazan, if you decide to accept this offer, you'll be the new manager for now. This was the suggestion of the former owner, Mr. Lazar." Farhi stared at me hard. "American Car is going to hire more mechanics and raise the wages of everyone who stays on with us. If you are approved after a trial period of three months, your contract will be revised again."

In point of fact, I had assumed the role of manager some months earlier, when Mr. Lazar stopped working, although there had been no official promotion. For a minute or so, I wanted someone to pinch me to make sure I wasn't dreaming. We all promptly declared that we wanted to stay on and thanked him for the opportunity. Then Leon Farhi looked me in the eyes and said, "Well, you're quite young! I hope you meet my expectations. They've spoken highly of you, and I think we're going to get along fine. Come to my office at American Car. Tomorrow morning at 10."

I just stood there, watching as the car drove off. My legs were shaking, and I was so happy I didn't know whether I should laugh or cry.

The next day, I arrived at the office of the American Car Company early. The secretary sent me directly in to the boss' office. Mr. Farhi asked me some personal and professional questions. Growing more at ease by the minute, I gave him straightforward answers, which apparently pleased him.

"If we want to keep this business successful, we need to have a first-rate body shop. You'll have to make sure we provide the best service in Sofia," he stressed. "I'm afraid the Germans and the new fascist government will interfere with our business and our lives, but I'm still hopeful that Bulgaria won't adopt anything like the Nuremberg laws now in force in Germany."

He was referring to the legislation approved by the *Reichstag* in 1935, declaring Jews and other minorities second-class citizens, pariahs with no political, civil, or any other kind of rights. The new laws were a serious threat to the freedom and even safety of anyone who wasn't an Aryan. In 1937, Herman Göring, the No. 2 man in the Third Reich, announced the end of Jewish participation in the German economy, and in 1938 he declared that the Jewish question was about to be "solved." In the midst of the ensuing persecutions and bloodbaths, some Jews were lucky enough to escape Germany, but many others – as the world would later learn – ended up in the gas chambers of Nazi concentration camps.

By then, these people had truly lost everything, even their identities; they had been reduced to numbers tattooed on their arms. There was no clemency for women or even for children. But at that point in time, in early 1939, none of this was known and so much was yet to come. Who could have imagined that the following six years would see the brutal deaths of more than 60 million civilians and soldiers on battlefields, in the ruins of bombed-out cities, and in concentration camps? Six million Jews would die in those camps, along with a horrifying number of Gypsies, Slavs, and even many Germans who were brave enough to stand up against National Socialism.

Under heavy pressure from Nazi Germany, the countries within the German sphere of influence were busy implementing laws similar to those of Nuremberg – and Bulgaria would be no exception. Bulgaria's pro-fascist politicians were favorable to the immediate enactment of Nazi-fascist laws, but opposition politicians, the art community, writers, the Church, and ordinary citizens had stalwartly resisted these attempts and thus forced their opponents to back down. All signs were that Bulgaria wanted to remain independent and distance itself from barbarian rule. At least that's how I saw things then.

As if he had read my thoughts, Mr. Farhi went on: "Don't think the Germans will give up so easily on the idea of doing away with us. I fear another great war will break out soon. With all these new weapons and technologies, it'll be the war of wars. The way things are going, Bulgaria will align itself with Hitler's Germany and then it'll be even harder to withstand anti-Semitic pressures. As unbelievable as it seems, we're going to align ourselves with the villains again. Our government leaders have the peculiar talent of always choosing the wrong side. Before Bulgaria finally loses the war, it's going to get real ugly."

Coming from such a powerful, successful man, this pessimistic prediction seemed exaggerated but still, it left me feeling uneasy.

In the following months, we had to recognize that the threat was real and the situation was worsening every day, despite Bulgarian resistance. Some time later, in early 1940, Mr. Farhi called me in for an urgent meeting. By then we had developed an easygoing relationship. When I saw that his children, Saul and Eva, were there with him, I realized something important was about to happen.

"Now that we're in the midst of war, I have to make a major change in the shareholder structure of my companies," he explained. "I've already made the needed changes to my tobacco export business, and now it's time to deal with the American Car Company. Do you see that blue folder of documents, Licco? You need to sign some of those papers in order to buy American Car from me and become the company's newest owner. I want to know if I can count on you."

"Mr. Farhi, of course you can count on me. You must have your reasons, but I don't really understand. I'm a mechanic, I don't know anything about business, and what's more important, I don't have any money and I'd never be able to pay you back." I was confounded.

"You'll understand soon enough," he replied. "In recent years, I've spent some time and money helping the resistance to fight fascist rule in our country. I've helped honest men – opinion makers – safeguard a vision of Bulgaria that's quite different from the one espoused by Hitler's lackeys. So far, these efforts have been successful – so much so that we've managed to keep our country somewhat independent. As to be expected, the Gestapo and Bulgaria's fascist rulers have been informed of my activities. Now the game is over, and I have to leave the country as soon as possible. My whole family is in danger. Their very lives are at risk. A German friend warned me of imminent peril; he's extremely influential and well-informed. As a matter of fact, I'm going to ask him to give you and your family a hand should things get any worse. You can trust him. Follow his instructions without asking many questions. To sum it up, in an effort to save some of my assets, I'm passing the bulk of everything I own to people I trust. Now has come the time to pass along American Car."

"But why me?" I asked insistently. "There's got to be a lot of other people who could run a company better than I can."

"Because I like you and trust you," he replied. "The contract stipulates a 10-year payment period. This just serves to justify the sale from a fiscal and accounting perspective. Well, if we're still alive, and as long as the fascists lose the war, I hope you'll return half of what remains of the company to me or my children. Doesn't that sound reasonable?"

"Of course. But I don't have any management experience, I'm only 20, and I'm afraid I won't know how to run the company," was all I could say.

"And I don't know if we're going to be alive," he responded in a sad tone. "Petrov, our accountant, will help manage things. You can trust him, and I've made it clear that we'll compensate him very well for his loyalty – that is, if anything is left."

It was obvious I didn't have anything to lose, but only to gain. So I agreed.

"*Mazel tov*, partner! Since there can't be any formal documents, I thought it'd be good to have everyone here who is involved, including my children, Saul and Eva, to witness our verbal agreement and shake your hand too."

Like old friends, Mr. Farhi and I exchanged a hug. I noticed that Saul and Eva were a bit tense, and I felt I should do something more than just express my thanks, like saying "For my part, I'll do everything I can to deserve your trust." But instead of talking, I looked Saul and Eva firmly in the eyes when I shook their hands. My intentions were more than sincere, and I felt they got the message.

After everything was duly signed and handed over to the company's lawyers, Mr. Farhi addressed me one last time: "Sound management has a lot to do with common sense, honesty, and simplicity. My recommendation is that you always rely on these principles in your business affairs. I have just one more important piece of advice: if you want to be successful, always pay your taxes on time. There are only two sure things in life: death and taxes."

And thus it was that at the age of 20, after the finest yet shortest class in business administration I would ever have in my life, I became a businessman, in a rapid and unexpected step up the ladder. During the course of my long life, I've followed Mr. Farhi's maxims religiously and never regretted it.

One week later, I received a message from Mr. Farhi. It was sent from Istanbul and advised me that he and his whole family were safe and on their way to the U.S. Just as he had feared, the Bulgarian parliament approved the lamentable

Defense Law for Protection of the Nation not long after that, in December 1940; Tsar Boris III sanctioned it one month later. Social-democrats, ruralists, communists, anarchists, intellectuals, and clergymen of all beliefs had fought bravely, but German pressure was ultimately too much. In 1941, Bulgaria joined the Axis – which then comprised Germany, Italy, and Japan – and officially entered World War II. For Jews like us, the terror was just beginning.

I could write page after page telling the story of this period, a sad one for Bulgaria and for me. But I've decided to share this part of my tale without delving into great detail – partially because the memories still depress me, and the shadows of the past return with a vengeance. We were stripped of our property rights and our individual freedom overnight. We were forced to walk down the street bearing yellow Stars of David on our chests so everyone would know we were Jews. We had to quickly relocate from large cities to rural areas since Jews could only reside in the interior. Everything we owned that could not fit into a 20-pound suitcase of clothing was confiscated and all Jewish businesses were seized, without any compensation.

Still not satisfied, and likewise under pressure from Germany, the fascists who had taken control of the country wanted to deport all Jewish people living in the Balkans to concentration camps in Germany and Poland. They managed to turn Bulgaria into a corridor for the passage of many Greek and Macedonian Jews to lands under Nazi rule. But when it came time to deport Bulgaria's Jews, the public outcry was so tremendous that the fascists had to back down.

The Bulgarians who wanted to help their disgraced Jewish friends showed moving creativity. The expression "two-way conversion" was coined as a reference to the fake conversion of Jews threatened with deportation, who would first convert to Catholicism and then switch immediately to the Bulgarian Orthodox Church, or vice versa. When the police tried to trace a convert's origins and prove that she or he was of Jewish descent, they would discover that the person was indeed a convert – but a Catholic who had turned away from the Eastern Orthodox Church and not from Judaism. Similarly, Orthodox New Christians could prove they'd been Catholic before. No document made any mention of these converts' Jewish heritage.

Led by the future *patriarch*, Bishop Stefan of Sofia, bishops in the country's largest cities threatened to engage in acts of civil disobedience, while some also offered their churches as a last refuge for the Jewish population. It is said that Cyril, Bishop of Plovdiv and later patriarch of the Bulgarian Orthodox Church, vowed to lie across the tracks to prevent the departure of transport trains. Meanwhile, the Deputy Speaker of the Bulgarian parliament, Dimitar Peshev, with the support of more than 40 other deputies, drove the government into such a tight corner that the fascists had to beat a swift retreat. All this, on top of an uproar from the general public – running the gamut from common folk to intellectuals – eventually forced the authorities to give up the idea of deportation, at least at that point.

The role that Tsar Boris III played in these events has never been clearly established. The fact is that if he had done more, the lives of many Greek and Macedonian Jews could have been saved. Yet it's also true that if he had done less, it is quite likely that we, Bulgarian Jews, would have followed our Greek and Macedonian coreligionists down the path to the gas chambers. Word has it that the Tsar disappeared (possibly to go hunting) precisely when the moment came for him to sign the documents authorizing the departure of the first train filled with Bulgarian Jews, ready for deportation. Thanks to this delay, the forces opposed to these barbarian acts had time to organize. As a result, the deportation was canceled and countless lives were saved.

More than six decades later, there are many who

would like to claim credit for miraculously saving the lives of Bulgarian Jews during World War II. The old adage holds true: victory has a thousand fathers, but defeat is an orphan. Although the precise facts will never be known, we were undoubtedly saved by a combination of factors, including the determination and bravery of the Bulgarian people, who refused to tolerate such inhuman acts in their country. And this is why the most notable Bulgarian representatives – Dimitar Peshev and bishops Stefan and Cyril – occupy a special place on the *Avenue of the Righteous among Nations* at the Yad Vashem holocaust museum and memorial in Israel.

Bright and early one morning, two days after the appalling law was enacted, police forces occupied the American Car Company, and I was not even allowed in to collect my few personal belongings and bid my employees farewell. Mr. Farhi's plan had failed, and my business career had ended as abruptly as it had begun.

In order to placate Hitler, the Bulgarian government came up with a compromise "solution" to the Jewish question: interning all Jewish men in labor camps. I must admit that these places were nothing like the German concentration camps that were to shock the world after the war. In the Bulgarian camps, Jews suffered much less. It is true that the work regimen was rugged, food scarce, and the cold brutal. Still, the vast majority of prisoners managed to survive. The peasants living in the vicinity of these camps, eyewitnesses to our anguish, would sneak us warm clothing whenever they could. More importantly, they'd bring us food, which helped save many lives. It was common for some of the guards – often retired police or army officers – to close their eyes to all this or even to aid us outright.

Fifty years later, when I was able to visit Bulgaria again, I looked for some of these peasants to thank. I didn't find a single one alive, but I did locate some of their family members.

Though they received me kindly, it soon became clear that they knew hardly anything about the internment in labor camps and even less about the noble deeds done by their parents and grandparents.

CHAPTER III

Labor camp

The new laws went into effect, and my brother and I were ordered to report to the train station. From there, we left for the village of Somovit, situated on the Danube River. We were to work on a road construction project, as well as on a bridge over the Vit, a smaller river. I'm convinced they chose Somovit, because it lay so close to the Danube, from where we could easily be shipped to lands under Hitler's rule. The Danube carried large numbers of Greek and Macedonian Jews to Vienna. And from there, to the gas chambers. The Nazis were still intent on their gruesome plan. During those years, the Danube was neither beautiful nor blue but storm-tossed and bloodstained.

My brother, David, and I were separated in Somovit, but he wasn't taken very far away. I received news of him almost every week, which was of some relief. At the age of 19, David was already an adult and no longer depended on me. Events had forced us to grow up before our time, adding years in a matter of days. At least my brother had finished junior high school, I told myself, and after the madness was over he could have a decent life.

The road we were working on lay in an inhospitable area, far from everyone and everything. We joked that it would link nowhere to no place. The work was heavy, and, malnourished as we were, it wasn't easy to endure 12 hours of grueling, physical toil in heavy heat or biting cold. Food was scarce – and bad to boot – and our clothes were poorly suited for hard labor. To our good fortune, most of the guards didn't really mistreat us. They were stern but rarely resorted to physical violence.

One gray day that was colder than usual, we had to quit early because our visibility was limited by fog and heavy snowfall. The cold was even getting to the armed guards, who opted to go to the tavern in the nearby village – after all, it was heated there, and they could drink to their fill. Meanwhile, back in our barracks, we tried any way we could to get warm, as a frigid north wind met with hardly any resistance and penetrated the flimsy walls of worn wood.

"Some men from another unit will be arriving today to spend the night here in these barracks," a guard informed us.

As we squeezed even closer together on the huge wooden platform that served as our bed, the new arrivals entered our barracks. When their faces peaked out from behind the rags that were shielding them from the cold, my heart leapt. I knew every single one of them. Not only were they from Sofia; they were from my neighborhood.

"Your brother's in the barracks next door," someone told me. I rushed out and soon found David, now with a long beard and a very skinny body. We hugged each other in silence. I could feel his tears run down my neck, and I saw that his face was stinging from the bitter cold and etched with the feelings our unexpected meeting had roused.

"That beard of yours would make an Orthodox rabbi proud!" I exclaimed, overcome by my emotions.

David grinned. His smile looked awfully familiar. "They look so much alike," I thought, fondly remembering our dad.

We talked about our lives and discussed the scant information we had about the outside world. It seemed the Germans were no longer winning as handily as before and that the Americans were finally helping the Russians and Brits, not only with weapons but also with troops. The latest news left no doubt that the war was indeed worldwide, with the Pacific in flames as well. It seemed like the forces of good had finally begun to confront evil on a level playing field. Thank God. This development kindled new hopes and provided some light at the end of the tunnel.

As soon as we were alone outside the barracks, at the mercy of the cold night air, David wasted no time telling me his plans: "Licco, I want you to be the first to know: I'm going to make a break for it."

"And go where, David? Where?" He had me really worried.

"With the help of some friends, I'm going underground, and I might join the armed resistance. I want to help bring down these fascist monsters. I can't take this life anymore."

I'd heard about the partisans – armed groups who engaged in ambushes and hid in the mountains. Their numbers included socialists, anarchists, communists, and some survivors of the Spanish Civil War, and they fought the Bulgarian police forces like heroes.

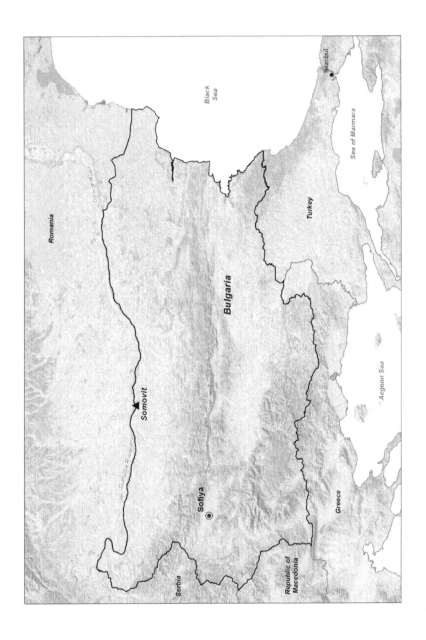

Apprehension gripped me. "That's extremely risky."

"It's just as risky as keeping your mouth shut in hopes these butchers will be merciful," he responded.

I'd always known that David was sympathetic to socialist and Zionist ideas and that many of his friends took part in these movements.

"The Soviet Union is going to win this war," David insisted.

With the United States in the fight as well now, this had become a real possibility. I had no argument, so I said nothing. In any case, I knew deep down that there was no point trying to stop my brother. His mind was made up.

We bid each other goodbye the next day, again without a word. I watched David and his small group move off into the distance and vanish into the fog. For the first time in many years, I cried. I cried for our lost youth, for fear about our uncertain future, and for those days of suffering. I cried for my dear brother, whom I might never see again. In the thick fog and relentless snow, my tears hardened to ice and went unnoticed. My brother was quick to make good on his promise. David did escape, and I heard nothing more about him.

It was late autumn 1943. The fallen leaves on the ground formed an endless carpet of color. Yet as lovely as the landscape was, it reminded us that another winter was on its way. We were all uneasy. We could feel ourselves growing weaker and weaker. For many of the men, their resistance had sunk to dangerously low levels. Salvator Mairoff was my closest friend in the camp. From the same neighborhood in Sofia, we'd known each other since childhood. He'd been sick for quite a while, fighting a high fever. One more winter under those conditions would be too much for his declining health. Even so, he was the most optimistic one in our group.

"This inclement cold will defeat the Germans. General Winter finished off Napoleon, and now it'll finish off Hitler. The Red Army is standing strong in Stalingrad, and it's starting to rule the battlefield. The Americans have taken on the Japanese in the Pacific, the Allies have just disembarked in southern Italy, and, as you must have noticed, even our guards are suddenly treating us better. I'm sure they've sensed their impending defeat. Rats always try to abandon a sinking ship. In next to no time, we can expect to be treated like welcome guests. Now we can count the days instead of the years. This nightmare is nearly over."

Turning to me, Salvator went on in excitement, "My friend, when this is all over, we're going to find ourselves some fine young ladies and get married. Can you just imagine? A nice bunch of kids? Me, I'd like a girl from a poor family, who has some job training and likes to ski."

"OK, Salvator, that makes sense, but why from a poor family?"

"Licco, my friend, think about the advantages of marrying a girl from a poor family today, compared to marrying one who comes from riches. A girl who's never known luxury doesn't have any great expectations, or bad habits, and it'll be easier for her to adapt to these hard times – even more so if she has an occupation and can help out. A girl who was born wealthy and then lost everything in the war, well, now she's poor, right? What's worse, she might cling to some expensive habits."

"Good God! You want to exploit your future wife!"

We laughed like we hadn't in a long while.

"Some day I'm going to make my biggest dream come true," Salvator said with conviction. "I'm going to stroll along Copacabana Beach, down there in Brazil, decked out in white pants and a Panama hat."

One of the fellows had gotten his hands on an old magazine with an article about that beautiful, peaceful beach, set in a breathtaking city in a sunny, exotic country. The magazine was one of the few things we had to read in the camp, and it got passed around. That was my first contact with Brazil.

"Right now, the sun is shining there, and it must be hot –nothing like this miserable cold," Salvator said in conclusion. Physically, Salvator and I were nothing alike. He was frail and weak, while I was strong and healthy as a horse. On the other hand, he had a terrific personality and was always in high spirits. But me –maybe because I was so worried about David– well, I tended to be glum and, on occasion, downright depressed. I helped Salvator with the heavy work and looked out for him as best I could when he was suffering from the cold or had a fever. In exchange, he rewarded me with heavy doses of optimism and good humor. We were veritable kindred souls during the brief but arduous months we spent together at the labor camp.

One time we were involved in an episode that could have had more serious consequences. One of the kindly peasants who supplied us with food and warm clothes whenever he could had slipped Salvator a bag of dried pea flour. We added water and put the mixture to boil in hopes of enjoying some soup. But we ended up with nothing but stiff, inedible dough. We added more water but still nobody liked our improvised dish – and we were starving! Disappointed, we tossed the remains to the chickens, which the guards raised in a corner of the camp and used to upgrade the quality of their own meals. Much to our surprise, some of the chickens turned up dead the next day.

We never understood why they died, but some of the guards suspected we had poisoned the poor things on purpose, and so they started looking into the matter and asking questions. Before they got to Salvator and me, we turned ourselves in and told them the whole truth. Considering our adverse circumstances, it would have been reasonable to expect some brutal form of punishment to be meted out as an example for others. Much to our amazement, however, our punishment could be considered mild: we were ordered to clean out the holes in the ground that served as makeshift toilets and also to tidy up the guards' quarters. After finishing these tasks, we went back to the barracks and to the fellowship of our friends, much to everyone's great relief. Salvator guffawed. "I bet the Germans lost the battle at Stalingrad! There must be some explanation for our guards' gracious benevolence. Now all we have to do is wait for the Soviets!"

I couldn't alleviate Salvator's pain or hold his feverish hand during the harsh winter of 1944 as I'd done the winter before. Years later, I found out he hadn't survived those especially frigid months. My memory still holds images of his face, lean as a starving child's, and his pale, almost transparent, skin. And I miss his contagious smile. Somehow, even though he's left us, Salvator stays with me, always walking alongside. Even now, whenever I have a problem, I ask for his advice –and he never lets me down.

The reason I wasn't with Salvator that winter was that I received a summons one day, a day that differed in no way from every other one at the labor camp – except for one detail.

"Licco Hazan! Licco Hazan! Present yourself at headquarters," I heard a guard shout.

In the nearly two years that I'd been at the camp, I'd never been called in for anything. We all knew that you could hardly ever expect a summons like this to end well, so the group huddled around me in worry. They gave me a warmer sweater, just in case, and lots of advice. I recall Salvator's words so clearly: "Licco, my brother, remember that you should never disagree or argue with those who are stronger. If they hurt you in any way, don't say a word and don't react, no matter what. Some thoughts can be really helpful in this type of situation. First off, remember that it'll all be over quickly, and the most important thing is to survive. Then, to make things easier on you, close your eyes and imagine your almighty jailer sitting on a toilet, his pants around his ankles, writhing from a violent bout of diarrhea. When things get tough, this formula will bring you a bit of relief and some immediate consolation. And believe me, it never fails."

My legs were shaking. I was filled with trepidation as I headed to the camp headquarters. There, next to the commandant, was a man I'd never seen before, in civilian dress.

"Licco Hazan, you're going to accompany Mr. Denev to Sofia."

"David! It must be about David," was my immediate thought.

"It must have something to do with car repair," the commandant said. "Aren't you a mechanic? When you come back, I want you to service our truck. I only realized we had a good mechanic on our hands when I saw your records now. Our truck is always breaking down."

The commandant gave Denev an envelope containing my documents, which had been stuck away in the camp files. He said sardonically, "Licco, don't do anything stupid, like trying to escape! We'll pick you up quick enough and that'll be the end of this bed of roses."

I didn't quite agree with the term "bed of roses," but I kept my mouth shut.

I managed to say goodbye to my campmates and return the pullover, which I wouldn't need anymore. Undoubtedly, they all envied the fact that I'd be leaving that hellhole and returning to Sofia, which now seemed like heaven itself. One by one, I hugged my long-suffering companions. I said my goodbyes to Salvator last.

"I'll be back in a flash," I said, choking up. Before my tears could fall, I hurried out of the barracks and didn't look back.

CHAPTER IV

Albert Göring

Half an hour later, I was seated in a luxury car headed toward Sofia. Denev liked to talk. Before long, my mysterious trip began to make more sense.

"I'm an engineer, and I work for Skoda. Are you familiar with it – the Czech auto plant that was taken over by the Germans?"

I certainly was. Skoda was an industrial giant that made cars, trucks, heavy power generation equipment, light weaponry, and even armored tanks.

"First, I'm going to see to it that you have a bath and get out of those filthy clothes. Early tomorrow morning, Chief Albert will talk to you."

My curiosity was piqued. "Who's Chief Albert?"

"He's my German boss, the director of Skoda. He lives in Prague, but he comes to Sofia every once in a while. I'm his right-hand man."

It was becoming increasingly clear that they needed my skills as an auto mechanic. That could be the only explanation.

Maybe if they saw me as a good tradesman, things would go better for me and I could still salvage something of my future.

"Chief Albert is a very important person. Even Tsar Boris receives him. He's a brother to that fellow Hermann Göring, the second most important man in Germany. Know who he is? The one that dresses like a peacock and is fond of all his medals!"

"My God, what can a guy like that want from me?" I wondered to myself. "Easy, Licco," I muttered under my breath. After all, I thought, things couldn't get any worse than they were. So I worked on keeping my calm and biding my time.

When we reached Sofia, Denev drove me to a modest inn, where I took my first hot bath in two years. I changed clothes and had dinner at a small restaurant chosen by Denev. Although I was famished, I could barely swallow the food in front of me. It had been a remarkable day. I was well fed, clean, and properly dressed, though the clothes they'd given me were a tad tight.

My next experience proved even better. I stretched out in the modest but comfortable bed in my room and reveled in that rare moment. I was neither cold nor hot, I had more room than I needed, nobody was snoring, and the covers seemed to caress me. I was treated so well that I felt safe. I could finally relax. They needed my services, and that might improve my lot – a great deal in fact. I slept like a baby.

The next day, I was taken to the Skoda offices, where the Albert Göring fellow was expecting me. I thought it was odd that they were showering so much attention on a simple mechanic, but I didn't have time to give it greater thought. I soon found myself alone with a dapper gentleman of average height. He was somewhat bald with a thin, well-groomed moustache and spoke softly in perfect *Hochdeutsch*. The man looked more like the Latin lover type than a stern German. I saw that he bore absolutely no resemblance to his much-feared brother.

"My name is Albert Göring, and I've called you in on the recommendation of Mr. Leon Farhi. I know that you've been interned in a work camp and that your brother escaped not long ago and joined the armed resistance. I don't need to tell you that you're in grave danger for the mere fact that your brother is an enemy, and even more so because you're a Jew. That's why we're going to fix you up with a new, legitimate Bulgarian passport, under a different name. We need to take your picture. This afternoon, we're going to get you a legitimate visa to Turkey, a neutral nation, where you'll be safe. The train to Istanbul leaves at 8 tonight. We have to hurry, because we don't have much time. You'll spend the day with Mr. Denev, and he'll drop you off at the train with other people who are in a similar situation and who also need to get out of Bulgaria as fast as possible."

So that was it. Farhi had made good on his promise to look out for me. This was the important man who had helped him get out of Bulgaria. I was so incredulous that I hadn't even opened my mouth. I'm sure my first question sounded somewhat ridiculous.

"Aren't I going back to the camp?"

"Of course not. And you're not going to wear that Star of David anymore. For all effects and purposes, you've got a new name and you're a wholly legitimate Eastern Orthodox Bulgarian. You'll hand your current documents over to Mr. Denev. You'll get them back when you're in Istanbul, along with a letter from Mr. Farhi. You'll also get further instructions from Mr. Denev, whom you can trust. It won't be easy to explain your disappearance, but I must honor Mr. Farhi's request. I have a great deal of admiration for the man. And all that's left for me now is to wish you good luck."

Still reeling, I thanked Göring. And that was the end of our conversation. It was the first and last time I'd ever see the man – a man I can call nothing but extraordinary. I owe my life to Leon Farhi and Albert Göring, who was the brother of the infamous Nazi butcher Hermann Göring.

After that, things happened so fast that I could barely keep up. I felt as if I were hallucinating, in a dream that would end at any moment. Not long after my photos were taken, Denev gave me my new documents, some Turkish money, and a piece of paper with an Istanbul address on it.

"There'll be people waiting for all of you at the train station, but I'm giving you this address just in case. Bear in mind that you're the leader of the group until you get there, so you'll have to help everyone else. Don't worry; everything's been well planned out. Now I'm going to take you to the Skoda garage and ask you to look over some cars. That way we can explain why you were here, and I'll have an alibi."

On the way to the garage, Denev told me the story of another Bulgarian who, like me, had fled the country using the fake documents of a German official that Albert Göring had gotten his hands on. The man was now safe and sound in Madrid.

"What's the lucky fellow's name?"

I was surprised to learn that he was a classmate of mine from the German school, Nissim Michael.

"Nissim was really lucky. So, has Mr. Göring helped a lot of others too?" I pressed him.

"In Bulgaria alone, more than 30. He's actually helped lots more folks in Romania, where Skoda has another office. Many Romanian Jews and some Hungarian and Czech Jews have taken the same route you'll be taking tonight. But I've got to admit that you've given us a lot more work; it's the first time we've gotten someone out of a labor camp."

"So these are experienced folks," I pondered out loud, feeling more at ease. Even so, I felt I had to warn my benefactor.

"I don't think the alibi is very convincing," I said as I checked out the cars.

"Maybe not," he replied. "But it's good enough for someone protected by Albert Göring."

After we finished up at the garage, I went back to the inn. Hours later, as instructed, I left alone, caught a tram, and then walked to the agreed-upon intersection. There, I climbed into a car driven by Denev.

"Now I can claim you escaped," he said with a grin.

We picked up three other people later: an older couple and a girl. The girl, by the name of Berta Michael, didn't appear to be more than 20. The couple looked familiar, and I discovered it was Rachamim Gerassi and his wife, Estreja. I knew several Gerassis. One of them, Rafael Gerassi, had been with me at the labor camp. On the other hand, I only knew two people from the Michael family: my friend from the German school, Nissim, and Elias Michael. Elias had been a race car driver before the war – quite unusual in those days – and I'd worked on his car a bit.

As we drew near the train station, Denev said a hasty goodbye. "From here on, you walk. I can't run the risk of being seen with you. Especially because Mr. Hazan (he pointed at me) has just escaped. By this time tomorrow, you'll be contemplating the Bosporus, while I'll be explaining the inexplicable to the Bulgarian police."

We were tense as we headed toward the station, where we mixed in with the crowd of passengers. We located our train and took our seats in a comfortable first-class cabin. Albert Göring didn't mess around! When I felt a climate of anxiety invade our compartment, I tried to look calm. The train pulled out of the station, and our journey began. As I struck up a conversation, I soon realized Berta was helping me keep things on an even keel, and I thanked her with my eyes. Since there weren't any strangers in our compartment, I asked her what she planned to do in Turkey.

"I don't have anyone in Bulgaria anymore. I'm an orphan. I love our country, and before the persecutions, I thought I'd live here forever. But now, that doesn't make any sense. I'm going to look up my aunt and uncle. They raised me, and they moved away from Bulgaria a little before this whole nightmare began. When they left, I decided to stay on and finish my accounting course. They passed those heinous laws not long after that, and, as a Jew, I couldn't get a passport anymore. At Mr. Leon Farhi's request – he's a friend of my uncle – Mr. Denev got in contact with me, and he arranged everything. My aunt and uncle live in Tel Aviv now, and I think that's where I'll go."

"I'm a good friend of Nissim Michael, (comma) and I know Elias, the race car driver, too. Are you cousins?"

"Yes, those good-fortuned fellows are my cousins. Elias, who's further removed, went to Canada some years ago, well before the persecutions. Nissim is my oldest uncle's son; my uncle passed away. Nissim just got out, with the help of Mr. Farhi as well. From what I've heard, he's safe and sound in Spain."

I wanted to hear Rachamim's story too. He'd managed to stay out of the labor camps because of his age. He told us he'd harbored Leon Tadjer Ben David, who had joined the partisans and, in the city of Ruse, blown up the fuel deposits that were supplying the German forces. Leon was discovered, arrested, and executed right after that. The police dismantled his clandestine cell and some of his friends were arrested, so it likely wouldn't be long before they'd uncover the group's most recent hiding spots. Fearing this would happen, Rachamim and his wife quickly went underground with the assistance of Bulgarian friends. They were lucky enough to be introduced to Denev, who organized their escape.

I took the opportunity to summarize my own story.

"I know you from synagogue," Berta said. "You always sit on the aisle, right? And you only come for the high holidays – *Passover, Sukkot, Rosh Hashana, Hanukkah*. You always get to *Yom Kippur* late, when we're just about to hear the *shofar*."

"No, no," I protested. "I never miss a *Kol Nidre*!"

It was a surprise that Berta knew me, whereas I didn't even remember her. Three or four years earlier, she'd still been a child, so I simply hadn't noticed her.

We sat there in silence for some time. The crew came around to check our tickets. It was a tense moment, but we handled ourselves well. Breathing a sigh of relief, I stepped out into the corridor to enjoy the breeze that was blowing through an open window. It was late autumn, and the air was quite cold. I couldn't help but think of the camp in Somovit. What were my barracks mates doing? And what about Salvator? And David?

The door of our cabin opened, and Berta came out to join me.

"Our traveling companions took some tranquilizers and are fast asleep. I came out to get some fresh air and stretch my legs. Am I bothering you?"

"Not at all."

It was then that I had a chance to notice her fine features and big eyes, which seemed to shine with their own light. The graceful lines of her face and her deep dimples, which appeared whenever she smiled, were truly striking. My impression was that she was a very fragile young lady who needed protecting.

"You have lovely eyes," I said without thinking.

She smiled. "I'm short and look frail, but I'm actually quite strong. I love numbers and logical reasoning. I've been working ever since I was a young girl. I started out teaching students who were having trouble in math, and then I studied accounting."

Her story sounded much like mine, and this sparked further conversation.

"Do you speak Ladino?" I asked.

"I speak and sing it." She started crooning "Avraham avinu, padre querido." It was a familiar song that evoked painful associations. Berta's voice was soft and musical. Her dimples deepened, enchanting me even further and leaving me a bit light-headed.

My experience with women had been limited and superficial. I'd never been involved in any truly serious relationship. I hadn't even known my mother, who died young. When I turned 16, some friends took me to a brothel, where I had a tryst with a prostitute that was as brief as it was unsatisfying. The only thing I remember is the heavy scent of cheap perfume and a dark, rather dirty place.

Later, while I was at American Car, I met Svetlana, a merry widow. I went out with her a lot, and she introduced me to truly gratifying sex. She was in her 30s and had fabulous curves. After the death of her husband, who had been much older, all she wanted to do was enjoy life. She was older than me by at least 15 years, but she kept herself in fine shape and was also one of the few women in Sofia who knew how to drive. I met Svetlana when I sold her a luxury car that had belonged to Leon Farhi. Averse to any serious commitment, she was adamant about keeping up appearances and protecting her good name. She appreciated my discretion, and so it was that we kept our relationship quiet. I have to admit that she was a top-notch teacher, and I proved to be an outstanding student. But this pleasant interlude was interrupted by my internment in the labor camp.

Four hours later, we reached the Turkish border, where

a Bulgarian guard checked our documents. Berta and I made a show of nonchalance, while Rachamim and Estreja were still drowsy from the effect of the tranquilizers; they scarcely noticed the guard.

"Have a good trip!" he said as he exited the compartment.

We entered Turkish territory and made it smoothly through immigration control. We had finally left any imminent danger behind. I hugged Berta, and we didn't say anything for a while. Then she smiled, and there were those dimples again. From that instant on, the chemistry between us was so strong and intense that it seemed like we'd known each other for years. I got lost in those big eyes of hers, and I felt a tremendous tenderness for the frail girl I held in my arms.

I was so very lucky. In less than three days, I'd gone from life in a labor camp to freedom. And on top of it all, I'd found the woman who would be the great love of my life. I was absolutely convinced.

CHAPTER V

Istanbul

The train slowed and pulled into Istanbul's central station. Our first days in the city were spent as tourists. Our host, Omer Aydin, owned a small inn a stone's throw from the Grand Bazaar and not far from other historical sites. Since our documents weren't legitimate, we couldn't do anything except explore the city in the daytime, when we could blend in with the crowd. There was so much to see, making it easy to understand why the Slavs had christened the city "Tsargrad," or "City of Kings." The Russian tsars had always had their eye on Constantinople – the name it was known by when it was the capital of the Byzantine Empire.

The city enjoys a matchless strategic location, right between Europe and Asia, straddling the Bosporus Strait and thus controlling access to both the Black Sea and the Sea of Marmara. Down through the centuries, Istanbul has attracted countless conquerors, each of whom imprinting a bit of their own culture on the city and its architecture. Ruins from the Byzantine Empire and the period of the Crusades can be seen all around. The city's impressive water supply system, Hagia Sophia and the Blue Mosque, the Roman Hippodrome, and Topkapi Palace are but a few examples.

ILKO MINEV

My grandfather, who spent a good part of his youth in Istanbul, always spoke of it with admiration and nostalgia. But even his most impassioned accounts paled in comparison to what I was seeing with my own eyes. The city breathed life, and despite the decline of the Ottoman Empire, it still exuded an air of might. Someone once said, and rightly so, that if the world were only one country, its capital would be Istanbul. I spent some of the finest, most decisive days of my life in that magnificent city.

Berta and I whiled away our time wandering the streets and admiring glorious views of the Bosporus. We stayed in the same inn as the Gerassi couple. Two other Jewish couples, both from Czechoslovakia, had arrived before us. The last of the rooms was occupied by Benbassat, a Romanian refugee. We had all received the vital assistance of Albert Göring, even though most of us had never met him personally. We needed to be discreet, because we'd entered Turkey on false documents and were still awaiting the arrival of our real ones, which we hadn't carried with us for obvious reasons. Turkish prisons had an awful reputation, and nobody wanted to get to know one firsthand. When one of us would ask Omer who was footing the bill for the inn, our meals, and other things, he'd change the subject. He was an affable person and a devout Muslim, who strove to please and protect us any way he could. The invisible hand of Farhi must have been behind it all, since the inn had only a few rooms and they were filled by us, penniless refugees.

Everything suggested that Omer was being paid for the services he rendered, particularly because he didn't seem to be a wealthy man. I recall that he was very proud of Turkey, which, while backward in some aspects, did have a secular system of government where religion didn't interfere with politics. Omer was a diehard fan of Kemal Ataturk, the man who managed to rouse Turkey from its slumber and modernize the country. Ataturk's guiding principles are respected and followed even today.

Omer gave us our real documents a week later and also introduced us to Greenwood and Bareau, two British women from the Red Cross. According to our host, these ladies would help us get our situation in order with Turkish officials. Greenwood and Bareau became a regular part of our lives and visited us almost every day. As far as we could understand, the Red Cross worked with other humanitarian agencies to get entry visas into countries that were accepting refugees. It was already a challenge to find a new homeland for all those people, and thousands more exiles would appear over time.

We had to fill out a lengthy questionnaire, where we stated our education and occupation, answered other personal questions, and indicated the country where we'd like to go. After a long wait, the Czechs who were staying at the inn were the first to obtain their visas, in their case to Australia. As Bulgarian refugees, our top choice was Palestine, which already had a sizable Bulgarian population. Miss Greenwood, however, explained that the British expected the situation there to grow complicated in the future and they were therefore hampering Jewish immigration to the region. Since we didn't have any other choice, we agreed to consider offers from other places, with the U.S., Canada, and Australia heading our lists.

Besides the aid I received from the British ladies, I found a gift among my Bulgarian documents: a letter from Mr. Farhi, just as Albert Göring had advised me in Sofia. I was moved when I opened and read it.

Dear Licco,

Welcome to Istanbul and to freedom. I am very grateful to you for all you did at American Car, and I wish you much success in your new life. You can always count on me if you ever need anything.

My advice is that you look for a new homeland and start your life over. Continue to be the honest, good-hearted man that I came to know.

You'll find my current address in the post-script to this letter. Keep me abreast of everything that happens to you.

Perhaps we shall meet again one day.

Your friend,
Leon Farhi

By then, the fact that I was courting Berta was public knowledge. We were inseparable from dawn to dusk, a look of absolute happiness pasted on our faces that seemed to shout: "I'm in love, and someone's in love with me!"

Gerassi, who played cards with us every night, didn't beat around the bush: "When are you two kids going to tie the knot?"

"As far as I'm concerned," I said, "tomorrow would be fine. Berta just has to say yes!"

Looking uncomfortable, Berta replied, "We don't have to be in such a hurry. Right now we're getting to know each other better."

Our card buddy smirked. "Back in my day," he said, "Estreja and I were in a big hurry. You couldn't date each other like you can today. No way you could go gallivanting about. But now – and of course the circumstances come into play – the two of you spend the whole day together. Even so, I bet Licco can't stand the wait anymore."

Everybody – Berta and I, no exception – joined in the hearty laughter.

Just a few days after this conversation, the British ladies gave us some surprising good news. Brazil, the Latin American country that had enthralled me ever since my time in the Bulgarian labor camp, was expediting visas for engineers and other technicians, including mechanics like me. According to the information provided by the Brazilian consul in Istanbul, visas for eligible candidates would be issued quite quickly. "My God! Brazil! Salvator will like this news," I thought.

I noticed the distraught expression on Berta's face. "Miss Greenwood," I asked, "do you suppose Brazil would be interested in a good accountant too?"

"From what I understand, their interest is quite specific," she replied. "Brazil is looking for people who have technical skills – but they don't have to be single. Why don't you two just get married and fix the problem that way? We still have to find out if you'd be going to Brazil right away. Since Operation Avalanche, when the Allies landed in southern Italy last September, the Mediterranean has been safe, but up until just a short while ago, the ocean route to South America was still a real target and quite dangerous. There were some German submarines that wouldn't even let merchant marine ships cross their paths. We have to find out if this remains a problem or if there are any ships sailing this route on a regular basis."

Berta and I took advantage of our plentiful time together by reading yesterday's papers, most of which written in English. Omer got them somehow from a lavish hotel. Armed with an English-German dictionary, we'd devour our precious source of information. A few days before our conversation with Miss Greenwood, we'd read an article about a naval battle that had taken place in the Atlantic. Germany's famous U-boats had given the country a huge advantage at the outset of the war, and they had ruled the seas for quite some time. It was only in early

1943 that the Allies managed to turn things around, using radar and sonar to locate subs and destroy them with depth charges. What had previously been a matter of general war news was now of vital personal concern to us. Years later, we learned just how many German subs had been wiped out: an astounding 783.

Miss Bareau asked with a smile, "Can we start planning a wedding? I know a rabbi who speaks Ladino."

Life in Istanbul had grown monotonous while we were waiting for things to be defined, but now the pace picked up and everything once again happened at the speed of light. Berta and I were married on January 10, 1944, complete with a quiet party at the inn. It was a very emotional occasion. Everyone cried. After years of tension and tragedy, these people were witnessing a happy event. I thought about David and Salvator, both of whom would have been part of our celebration in times of peace, and I said a prayer for them.

We received our temporary documents a few days later, bearing permanent visas for Brazil. On January 26, 1944, we set sail from Istanbul aboard the *MS Formosa*. We would first go to Gibraltar, where we would catch another ship – the *Jamaïque* – that would take us to the port of Santos and to our new life in Brazil.

Our journey to Gibraltar was the honeymoon for which we had so longed. It was a gift from Miss Greenwood and Miss Bareau, who dipped into their own pockets to cover the difference between the cost of our fare in steerage and second-class tickets on the *Formosa*. The men and women were lodged in separate quarters in steerage, which wouldn't have given us the privacy we desired. I'm so grateful for the glorious days we spent on our honeymoon. To our good fortune, the sea was calm and the temperatures balmy in the Mediterranean. We were like two little kids at

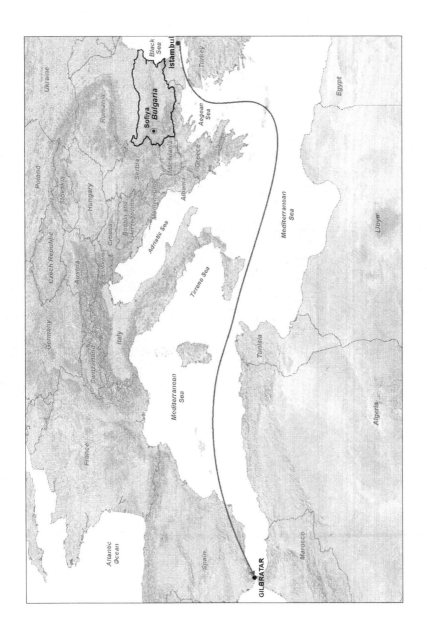

long last discovering their bodies, joyfully, spontaneously, and without any shame or fear. The sex was merely a complement, an extension of our feelings, and this made it all the more wonderful. The trip to Gibraltar lasted just over a week, but it remained in our memories as the happiest, most relaxing time of our lives.

Before we departed Istanbul, Omer handed us some money to tide us over during our first weeks in Brazil, along with tickets in steerage from Gibraltar to Santos, bought with funds from Farhi. Unlike our smooth sailing through the calm waters of the Mediterranean, our voyage from Gibraltar to South America was fraught with trials and tribulations. Going through my papers, I came across my travelogue from the trip on the *Jamaïque*. Although few in number, these pages describe our journey surprisingly well.

CHAPTER VI

Honeymoon aboard the *Jamaïque*

Jamaïque, February 7, 1944
(200 miles west of Gibraltar)

The *Jamaïque* is a 10,000-ton ship with a nominal cruising speed of 10 knots. I say "nominal" because it became clear right away that the ship cannot even do eight. It carries passengers and cargo between Europe and South America, and its scheduled route is Gibraltar, Dakar, Rio de Janeiro, Santos, Montevideo, and Buenos Aires. There are 1,000 people on board: 200 crew members, 100 first-class and 100 second-class passengers, and 600 in steerage. Right at the entrance, we were shocked by the filth and smoke that pervaded steerage. Our dismay only deepened when we saw our accommodations. We'd known we wouldn't have comfortable cabins, but what confronted us was much worse than we'd expected.

I'm staying in the smaller, men's dormitory, where a hundred bunk beds are squeezed on top of one another. The bunks are so low that you can't sit on the bottom one, and you can only climb into bed by crawling from one bunk to the other, which forces us all to get in and lie down as fast as we can. Still, my spot is one of the better ones, because it's close to a porthole and I get some fresh air. The real trouble comes when someone needs to use the bathroom in the middle of the night. It's a huge bother, and so everyone tries to hold it in as best they can. Berta's cabin has an even tinier porthole, (comma) but the whole women's area is smaller. There are just 11 bunks and five cribs, which can only be wedged in once most of the women have lain down. It's essentially impossible to get up in the middle of the night, no matter how pressing the need. And some of the women sleeping there are pregnant!

Worse than our lodgings are the bathrooms and laundry area. The crew pours some kind of disinfectant in there four times a day, but the smell is still horrendous, and it's almost impossible to stay in there. Nonetheless, long lines of sad, weary, broken, demoralized people form at the entrance. The capacity of the toilets falls far, far short of the needs of the 600 poor wretches in steerage. God, how I miss the *Formosa*!

The first hours on board were dreadful. Quarrels were always breaking out – over space in the dormitories or space in the canteen or on deck. As soon as the *Jamaïque* hit open waters, another trial began: nausea struck. It hit us as high waves rocked the ship back and forth. We soon couldn't find a single spot that hadn't been fouled with vomit. The stench was unbearable!

So it came as no surprise when the captain ordered a thorough cleaning of the ship, summoning the crew along with those who stood to gain the most: the passengers in steerage. Armed with cleaning supplies, we managed to make things quite a bit better. The byproduct was a ceasefire in the constant fighting, and it's been clear that we're gradually adapting to this state of affairs, where each of us has but a tiny space.

It's still cool in the mornings and at night, but you can tell we're getting closer to the equator. Berta has preferred to spend nights on the deck; the heat hasn't let her sleep. In the daytime, we've got a little spot on the deck, right across from the door to one of the officer's cabins. These places are generally off limits but when the officer, Joaquim (he's Portuguese and can understand our Ladino), saw a small mob of people fighting for a corner, he kindly invited us to occupy that prized location.

In the afternoon, someone in first class plays piano music that drifts over to us. It's so wonderful! Berta and I can be together most of the time, and once in a while we even get to sneak a kiss or two. Still, having sex in steerage on the *Jamaïque* is unthinkable, and I've quickly realized that having my beloved wife next to me without being able to touch her is somewhat akin to medieval torture.

You can hear all the languages and dialects imaginable on the ship: *Yiddish*, German, Russian, Turkish, Arabic, Greek, Dutch, French, Czech, Bulgarian, Serbian, Spanish, Hungarian, Portuguese, English, and Scandinavian tongues. I've never witnessed anything that resembles the tower of Babel so much!

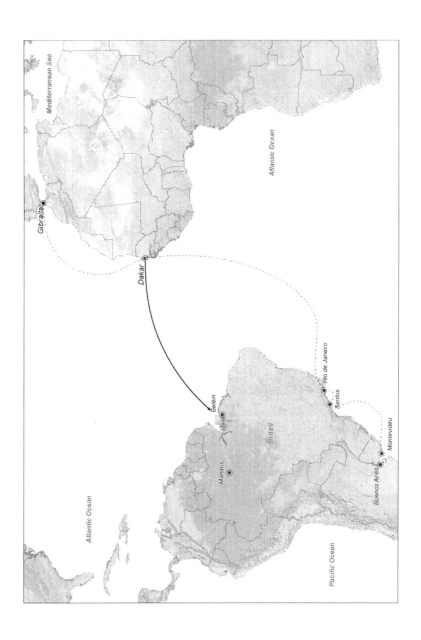

Jamaïque, February 11, 1944
(300 miles north of Dakar)

Four more days have gone by, and today marks our eighth aboard the *Jamaïque*. The wind started up yesterday and the waves are taller, but now we're adjusted and few passengers are seasick. We walk around with our legs spread apart, and the soup sloshes around in our bowls, but that's about it. Overall, we're feeling better, and some folks are even dabbling in a protest over the poor quality of the food. As a result, things have actually improved a bit, but we don't know how long this will last. The weather changed today. There's a bitter wind that has forced us to seek shelter inside, where life is so much harder.

After being packed together in the ship for so long, groups based on language and culture have begun to take shape. Before boarding, most of us had survived dramatic and even frightening moments; we've often heard such accounts that are both amazing and dreadful.

We spend hour after hour playing chess and backgammon. We're virtually isolated from the rest of the world. The captain issues a brief bulletin every three or four days, with news that's come in over the radio. It's not much, but we all look forward to it. There's a small library on board, and Berta came up with the idea of checking out some English and Spanish books in the hopes of better learning these languages. One person in the group tries to read a sentence aloud, and then we translate it together, with the aid of a dictionary. Sometimes the results are totally ridiculous and hilarious, providing lots of laughs and fun. This makes the time pass much faster.

It's a shame we sailed by the Canary Islands at night. All we could make out were some lights. Still, it was exciting to feel close to that other world, so much better than ours, far from the war and the ordeals of a crowded ship. A thick fog hangs over everything today, so we haven't seen the coast of

Africa yet, just some small fishing boats dancing in the ocean waves. Amazing! It makes us dizzy just to watch! We're dying to get to Dakar and off the ship, even if only for a few hours. I want to buy some fruit for Berta, who hasn't been eating as well as she should. I worry about that.

When we leave Dakar, I'm going to write a little about our brief African experience. If I don't write things down now, I fear these memories will be lost amid the emotions awaiting us in our new homeland of Brazil.

I should mention that someone got sick from the heat inside his cabin yesterday, but thankfully he recovered quickly. On the other hand, a 7-month-old baby couldn't beat a high fever and died.

Jamaïque, **February 15, 1944** ### (9°N, 21°W, near Dakar)

The day before yesterday, after lunch, we got our first glimpse of the coast of Africa. As we drew closer to land, small fishing boats with rectangular sails approached the ship. We caught sight of buildings as well: some long barracks, which must have housed soldiers, and many small huts in indescribable shapes and colors. It's all very different and exotic, even more so because the whole coast is blanketed with lush palm trees.

We had almost reached the main port when we spied an island with military forts on it. The *Jamaïque* had to stop there first to comply with all the debarkation rules, and the list must not be a short one – it took hours. Once we'd dropped anchor at the port, Berta and I rushed to the post office to mail some letters and postcards to friends and relatives. Before we'd even realized, it was 7 in the evening and we had to head back to the ship. We didn't get to see anything of the city. We barely had time to buy fruit.

In Istanbul and Gibraltar, we'd seen some black people, which is something new for Berta and me. In Bulgaria, there weren't any black or Asian people; we'd only heard about them through books and movies. Well, in Dakar, we saw a lot of black people. They wear clothing sewn from colorful prints, and it makes for an incredible picture. Some of them looked very healthy and had the athletic silhouettes of Greek gods. But most of them were sick and quite debilitated. Some walked about dressed impeccably in white, whereas others wore nothing but dirty, torn rags.

On the way back to the ship, we were surrounded by a crowd of people trying to sell us articles made of fake ivory, handicrafts of crocodile leather, and other things of dubious origin. They were hawking food as well, like bananas and chocolate, which they wanted 150 French francs for – and then they'd unabashedly turn around and take 50. You had to patiently bargain them down until you arrived at a relatively fair price. A lot of them wanted to buy dollars and would offer 50 francs but actually pay as much as 150.

After much haggling, I ended up buying a kind of folding chaise lounge for Berta. I paid 500 francs. Lots of other folks bought the same type of chair, which looked like it would be quite useful on the trip. Back at the ship, we found out that some had paid 1,200 francs for the very same article, while others had paid 400. It was comical to watch the reaction of those who discovered they'd been cheated and had thrown their money down the drain.

Returning to our onboard routine, we soon discovered that cabins are awful in the tropical heat. So we had to fight tooth and nail to defend our space outdoors, the one we'd conquered much earlier when it was still cold. Joaquim helps us out as best he can.

Some idiot, in the hopes of securing space outside, spread the rumor that we'd be running into snowstorms at the equator. It's funny to see how many believe him. Some folks have even given up their place on the dock in fear of the cold. Good God! How ignorant can you get?

With the heat rising steadily, the bathrooms reek so much that you've got to plug your nose before you go in. It seems like the ship switched over to a very poor-quality fuel bought in Dakar. The smokestack blows out a steady stream of sparks, and everything around us is covered in dark soot. This holds true for the passengers as well; even after a bath, we're still dirty and stinky. And thus we sail oh so slowly toward the equator, counting the minutes of this torment.

Jamaïque, February 21, 1944
(600 miles east of Brazil)

I'm madly in love with Berta. She's everything I could have dreamed of and so much more. On top of my love, I have a profound admiration for this little bundle of courage, who charms everyone with her cheerful disposition, optimism, and common sense. She's tireless when it comes to helping anyone who needs it. Since she's so well organized and efficient – without being pretentious but always in a good mood and with a smile on her lips – everybody likes her and confides their problems to her. As a result, lots of folks on the ship know us, and most of the passengers are friendly to us. I'm absolutely certain that when Salvator meets Berta, he's going to adore her. She's so much like the girl he dreamed of meeting some day.

As to be expected, we didn't run into any snowstorms when we crossed the equator. To the contrary, we had a great reprieve: a breeze! It's made the temperatures feel much more agreeable, especially at night. There are at least 80 of us on our deck now. Most speak German, French, or Spanish, but we also hear Russian, Italian, and English. Everybody gets along. In a year like 1944, this is ironic, as the enmity and hatred between our nations have culminated in the deaths of so many on the battlefronts. Here, to the contrary, we help each other out as best we can. We watch over our neighbor's space when he or she goes to the bathroom. These are little things, but they mean a great deal.

It's almost over, and Rio de Janeiro awaits us. It's been so long since Berta and I have had a little privacy…! Just a little more patience, Licco. A little more!

Jamaïque, February 29, 1944 (still far from Brazil)

We're still quite a ways from Rio de Janeiro. We're actually closer to the Brazilian coast now, but much farther north than our route was supposed to take us. On the night of February 24, we were suddenly hit by a storm, the likes of which I'd never seen. The waves crashed across the deck and swept everything out of their way. For minutes at a time, they looked like gigantic lips engulfing the entire ship. In panic, we sought refuge inside, where we watched the raging sea. The tossing of the ship was terrifying. Nobody's stomach could take it. Everybody got sick. All around you could hear desperate prayers in every possible language.

The *Jamaïque* was crawling along very slowly when the lights suddenly went out. Everything went black, and a weird sound came from the engines. The captain practically lost control of the ship, so he tried to use what little power the engines had left to head straight into the waves. As a good mechanic, I could tell from their sound that the engines were close to dying. Without them, it would only be a matter of time before the enormous waves pounded right into the side of our defenseless vessel. Then we'd certainly go down.

I warned the others in our group, and we all rushed to grab a life vest. Luckily, we managed to prepare for the worst before everybody else grasped how serious things were. We decided to stick together the whole time, especially to defend our life vests should the ship start to sink and pandemonium break out. All signs were that there weren't enough life vests for all the passengers, and it was important to be prepared for any possibility.

This torture lasted nearly six hours before the storm finally let up. At almost the same time, the engines of the *Jamaïque* ground to a halt. "The hand of God," I thought. If the engines had gone out just a little bit earlier, we would have been done for.

Once the ship stopped, the heat became unbearable. The smell of vomit was overpowering too. The cleaning supplies, which had been scarce before, were wholly depleted now. Without any kind of disinfectant and everything on the ship in deplorable shape, it was impossible to accomplish any kind of reasonable cleanup. The storm had been democratic, hitting the first-class passengers as well, and now there wasn't a single spot that was clean. Yesterday afternoon, (comma) we caught sight of a ship that would answer our distress call. But our joy was short-lived. It was a cargo ship sailing under a Panamanian flag, and it couldn't really do much for us. A few crewmembers came aboard, but they didn't stay long, perhaps because of the stench that had permeated the whole place by then, even first class. They returned with some barrels of drinking water - which we were beginning to run out of - and lots of cleaning supplies, so that we could set about cleaning the whole ship over the coming days – as part of a huge hygienization project. The captain just informed us that a Brazilian tugboat will get here soon and tow us to the nearest port. Hallelujah!

Jamaïque, March 1, 1944
(on our way to Belém)

The Brazilian tug just got here, bringing with it more water and new hope. We're not going to Rio de Janeiro anymore but to the nearest port, Belém, which means Bethlehem in Portuguese. We didn't even know there was a city by this name in this corner of the world. The storm and the ocean currents pushed the *Jamaïque* west, near the mouth of the Amazon River. Neither the name nor the place matters. At this point, all we want to do is get off the ship, take a bath, change into some clean clothes, and eat a good meal!

Jamaïque, March 3, 1944

We're almost there! Almost there! During the day, seagulls announced the approach of land. It's night now, and by the light of the full moon, we can tell we're sailing along the coast. South America is just over there. Someone told us we're passing the island of Marajó, on the Amazon River, and we'll reach Belém early in the morning. Nobody onboard can sleep. We're all so excited.

CHAPTER VII

A new life in Belém

The Lord said to Abram, "Go forth from your native land and from your father's house to the land that I will show you."
Genesis 12:1

We finally docked and got off the ship. While we were still at sea, it had become evident that there would be no short-term repair for the *Jamaïque*, so our debarkation was definitive. Some of those who could afford it to got their hands on tickets to leave for Santos within a few days.

Realizing we had to make a decision, Berta pulled me aside for a quick talk. With a twinkle in her eye, she pointed out that no one was waiting for us in Santos and that it would be worth staying in Belém for at least a few days. I agreed on the spot. Our honeymoon had been interrupted more than a month earlier, and we could pick up where we'd left off. Sharing the same ulterior motive, Berta and I exchanged a naughty look. It was wonderful to have a wife who was also a lover.

Debarkation was a horrific sight – a thousand long-suffering souls, stinky and exhausted, abandoning a ghost ship. People got off carrying their sparse belongings and bent to kiss the Brazilian soil. Even the customs officials were moved by the scene.

One last look at the sad, deserted *Jamaïque*, and Berta exclaimed, "*Jamaïque jamais!* Never, ever again!"

As I think back on our time aboard the *Jamaïque*, only now do I realize how hard the trip had been on her. A new life had just begun, in a new world and a new homeland.

"For God's sake, where's the nearest hotel in this town?"

With our most pressing issue taken care of and after a restorative night's sleep in a real bed, we went out to see Belém. We quickly discovered that the city was hot. Very hot. And quite muggy, even when there was a breeze. The humidity must have been extremely high. It rained a lot, but the warm water didn't seem to get anything wet.

We spent the day perspiring hard, our clothes damper from sweat than from the rain. In the late afternoon, we returned exhausted to our inn, which had the suggestive name "Paraíso," Portuguese for "paradise." We had a bit of trouble deciding on our food, because the cuisine was so exotic. It struck us how everything was very cheap, yet many basic things were hard to find.

Belém was a pretty town. There was an abundance of green, with mango and other leafy trees shading the main streets and avenues. It must be dangerous to walk under them during the times of the year when they hang heavy with fruit. There were many varieties we'd never seen before. Some of them were delicious, but others were so different that we couldn't decide whether we liked or hated them. A new world indeed.

We were amazed by the number of large, lovely homes, some of which being veritable mansions. Most of the buildings, however, were in a shoddy state of repair, and many stood empty.

Clearly, the town had seen better days not so long before.

The calmness of the locals also caught my attention. They were never in a rush. During one of Belém's typical rains – which fall at the same time every day – we went into a little café and ordered some coffee, served strong, sweet, and in a tiny cup. When it came time to settle the bill, we learned that one of the people with whom we'd chatted a bit at the door had paid our tab and then up and left, just like that. Not that a big sum was involved, but this kind of action was quite different from what we were accustomed to experiencing.

"These folks are so kind and generous," Berta said. "They've won my heart with their easygoing ways and basic goodness. You can tell they haven't suffered as much from the war here."

We later came to understand that this was only half true. Almost everything, from bread to electricity, was rationed or simply couldn't be had because of the war. The fan that should have provided some relief from the heat in our room stood still at night. We would lie there in the dark, drenched in sweat, until a soft breeze helped us fall asleep.

In 1944, Belém had a population of a little more than 200,000. Most of its inhabitants were poor, few enjoyed an easy life, and fewer yet had cars. Given my profession, this was an important consideration. Because you couldn't get parts, there was only a market for skilled, creative mechanics. I spotted a good business opportunity there.

"Do you think it'd be worth looking for work here, or should we continue on to Rio de Janeiro?" I asked my wife.

Berta thought a minute before saying, "I'd like to spend a little more time here. I'm still seasick from the *Jamaïque*, and I couldn't face another ship. Anyway, I'd like to learn more about the local cuisine. I love the taste of *tucupi, jambu,* and other local spices. They lend a curious indigenous touch to Pará's cuisine. I don't even know all their names yet. We should spend some more time at the dockside market too, that place called Ver-o-Peso. I read the other day that it's stood on the banks of the Guarajá River since 1625. It was a tax collection house back then, where all the goods were weighed so they could calculate the taxes owed to the Portuguese Crown. Thus its name, 'see the weight.'" Berta had been captivated by the local culture.

"Did you notice how many different kinds of fish they have at the market? All typical of this region, and we know hardly a thing about it," I said, caught up in excitement about life in Belém. "And they're so tasty. Those two varieties called the smooth and the acoupa weakfish could easily be served in the most expensive restaurants in Paris."

Berta had also been seduced by the aromas of Belém. This was partly because our month aboard the foul-smelling *Jamaïque* had left us rather traumatized about odors.

"There are so many herbs and handcrafted scents and perfumes. Despite the stifling heat, most people smell like they'd just stepped out of the bath. There must be markets all over the world for these fragrances," added Berta.

Not too long after this, we would realize that we'd actually be staying much longer in Belém and that Berta's nausea was not caused by our time on the *Jamaïque* but by our first son, Daniel.

* * * * *

We quickly got a better feel for the city and its life. We made some friends and were told that the *Sha'ar Hashomayim* synagogue was a fully functioning house of worship. This was a pleasant surprise. They say that wherever there's a fairly decent-sized economy, you'll find Jews. But in Belém? Frankly, we hadn't expected that.

The next night was the start of *Shabbat*. Dressed in our best, we headed to synagogue. We were surprised at how many people were there. My God, there was a large community in Belém!

At Sha'ar Hashomayim, as in all traditional Sephardic synagogues, the women spent the service on the upper part, on a sort of balcony, while the men remained in the lower part, facing the *Hekhal*, or ark, where the sacred Torah scrolls are kept. The prayer was so familiar that I felt as if I were in Sofia. But my heavy perspiration reminded me that I was in the tropics and far, far from Bulgaria.

I found an empty chair and sat down. Since synagogue is also a place for socializing, it wasn't long before a tall, dark man who looked about my age offered me a Shabbat prayer book and sat down next to me. Once he felt confident that I was familiar with the service, my neighbor displayed an interest in talking. Outsiders are a rarity in Belém, and it was obvious that my new acquaintance was curious.

"Shabbat *shalom*! I'm Moyses Bentes. I see you're new here."

"Shabbat shalom! My name's Licco Hazan. Please, speak slowly," I said in Ladino. "I don't speak Portuguese yet, but I do understand a great deal."

"Your Spanish helps a lot."

"Actually, I'm speaking Ladino. It seems it's very close to Portuguese."

Bentes grew even more interested, and he proceeded to shower me with questions.

"Ladino? Are you Sephardic too? I bet you're from Syria or Egypt. Are you here on business?"

"No, I'm not here on business. My wife, Berta, and I are Sephardic Jews from Bulgaria. We came in last week on the

Jamaïque, the ship that's still in the harbor." I pointed to Berta. I was happy to see her engaged in a lively conversation with some other women.

"That's interesting. You're actually communicating quite well already. And from the looks of it, your wife is too. I see she's talking to my wife, Débora, and some other friends of ours. What do you do for a living?"

"I'm an auto mechanic. All modesty aside, I'd say I'm a good one."

"A mechanic..." He mulled this over. "Could I invite you to have dinner at our house after synagogue? We'll have a Shabbat meal with the whole family. It'll be very simple."

That's how I met Moyses, a dear friend whom I miss very much. We were friends for more than 60 years. God took him a few years back. He was the one who introduced us to the Jewish community in Belém and told us the extraordinary history of the immigration of Moroccan Jews to the Amazon.

That same night, we learned that Belém had been a very wealthy city in the early 20th century, when the Amazon was at the peak of its prosperity and economic euphoria, thanks to the rubber industry. Commercial-scale rubber tapping began in 1850 and reached its apex in the first decade of the 1900s, when the Amazon region produced an astounding 345,000 metric tons of precious latex. This represented an incalculable fortune back then, and it turned the rubber barons into some of the richest men on earth. But the euphoria was short-lived. In 1910, the Amazon felt the devastating impact of the innovative rubber plantations in Malaysia and Ceylon, and later in Indonesia as well. This explained how a city that had been so prosperous for several decades had fallen into decay.

"Do you want to learn a little more about Brazil? I'll lend you a very good book," said Moyses. "It's called *Brazil, Land of the Future*."

When I saw the book, I couldn't contain my surprise. "Stefan Zweig! I've read him. I loved his novel *Amok*, and another one too – unless I'm mistaken, the title is *Fear*. He's one of the most brilliant writers of this century. I wasn't even aware that he was familiar with Brazil or that he had written about it."

"He not only wrote about it – he lived here, and he's actually buried in Petrópolis, a town near Rio. He and his wife committed suicide a little while ago. It was a huge scandal that saddened the whole country."

I opened *Brazil, Land of the Future* and leafed through it. The first edition had come out three years earlier, in 1941. One sentence in particular struck me; it was a precise, sensitive description that captured the essence of the colorful country of Brazil. I read it aloud: "Whereas our old world is more than ever ruled by the insane attempt to breed people racially pure, like racehorses and dogs, the Brazilian nation for centuries has been built upon the principle of a free and unsuppressed miscegenation, the complete equalization of black and white, brown and yellow."

"I love it," exclaimed Berta. "I want to be part of this colorful chaos!"

During our pleasant dinner with the large Bentes family, we heard more details about the incredible Jewish exodus, first from Spain and Portugal to Morocco, and then from Morocco to the Amazon. We already knew a little about the Jewish people's dramatic flight from the Inquisition, but we had no idea that such a large community existed in Morocco.

We learned that Moroccan Jews, like Bulgarian Jews, trace their roots to the Iberian Peninsula. The persecution of the Jews in that region of the world was at its worst in the late 15th century. In the Jewish quarters known as *Juderias* in Spain, and as *Aljamas* in Portugal, life hadn't been easy before then, but it was only with the systematic persecution fomented by the Inquisition that fleeing the Peninsula became not only necessary but a matter of life or death.

In 1492, Spanish Jews were the first to exit en masse. Portuguese Jews were next, expelled by King Dom Manoel in 1496. The bulk of these two groups chose Morocco as their destination because of its geographic proximity. Others ventured into the Ottoman Empire, which then included Egypt, Syria, and the Balkans. The third choice was the Netherlands, owing to its racial and religious tolerance. From there, some set sail for Recife, accompanying Maurício de Nassau's invading forces. When the Dutch were subsequently driven out of Pernambuco, they sailed to the Caribbean and scattered about the islands. Another contingent continued on to North America and settled in what is now the city of New York.

Three hundred years later, in the early 1800s, which were also the days of Napoleon and his empire, Moroccan Jews initiated a new exodus, this time to the Amazon. It was triggered by various political, economic, social, and religious factors –. Poverty was widespread in Morocco back then, but Jews were the poorest of the poor. Sanitary conditions in Moroccan cities were as bad as they get. People were assailed by the plague and other epidemics, and hunger was common to all Moroccans, Jewish or otherwise. Moreover, a portion of public officials and the community at large displayed great animosity toward Jews, which helps explain why so many members of the community joined the second exodus.

But why the Amazon? There are a number of theories. The major transformations then occurring in the young country called Brazil had a lot to do with it, such as the opening of the ports to the rest of the world in 1808, Emperor Pedro I's termination of the Inquisition in 1821, the enactment of the Imperial Constitution in 1824, the freedom of religious expression that came with the Proclamation of the Republic of the United States of Brazil in November 1889, and, lastly, the opening of navigation on the Amazon River to foreign countries, granted by Emperor Dom Pedro II in 1876.

If you factor in both scenarios – the instability of life in Morocco and the dazzling outlook in a new Promised Land, a new Canaan – it's easy to understand the staggering exodus that made a major contribution to the Amazonian melting pot.

Back in our room at the Paraíso after our Friday night Shabbat dinner, we couldn't fall asleep. It was a lot to absorb in one day. In our darkened room, Berta and I stayed up talking until the wee hours. We were incredulous to have heard that there was yet another synagogue in Belém, *Essel Abraham*.

"All told, there must be more than 500, maybe 600 Jewish families in Belém alone. Not counting other families that live in smaller towns in the interior, right in the heart of the forest," Berta said, marveled by what we'd heard.

"Moyses also mentioned a large community in Manaus, a city some distance from here, a bit smaller than Belém. It's a little more than 900 miles from here if you take the Amazon River. Even farther away, in Peru, there's the city of Iquitos, which is home to Jews from Morocco too. It's really hard to believe."

We pondered what it must have taken for those people to reach their destinations. How did they travel up the mighty river against the current with no engines to rely on, just oars and the wind? How had they fared, not only in the big cities but in the huge, wild lands of the Amazon? They had inarguably played important roles in what is known as the first Rubber Battle, which began in the mid-19th century and ended around 1915, according to Moyses Bentes.

You couldn't have invented a more bizarre history. No doubt about it, real life is even more imaginative and fantastical than anything the human mind could ever dream up.

The next day, (comma) we bid farewell to the last of our cross-Atlantic traveling companions who had remained in Belém and at the Paraíso. They were going to continue their trip to a big city in southern Brazil called São Paulo. Góran was Croatian and had been our chess instructor aboard the *Jamaïque*. Their little girl had taken sick at the end of the trip, and that's why he, his wife, and the child had been forced to stay in Belém. We'd lent them a hand now and then when they couldn't communicate in Portuguese. Now the baby was fine, and it was time to go. When they came to hug us goodbye, Góran pulled me aside and said, "Licco, I want to tell you something important. You two are the first Jewish people I've ever known. I had the wrong idea; I thought I didn't like Jews. Now I know you're folks just like us, and I'm so happy and grateful that we met. I hope we'll meet again someday, so I can teach you an opening by the world's greatest chess master, *Capablanca*. He's a genius."

"At least the *Jamaïque* was good for something," I said, moved by his words.

We embraced, and they left.

This exchange has stuck in my memory all these years. It's a demonstration of how prejudice against blacks, Jews, Arabs, and any other ethnic group or nationality is a product not of facts or knowledge but of ignorance or fear of anything that's different.

* * * * *

Now that we had decided to stay in Belém, it was time to look for work. Berta visited a number of companies, but it didn't take long for us to see that Belém had plenty of unemployed bookkeepers. We realized we'd have to stop spending such a big portion of our meager funds on lodgings and rent a small house instead.

Fortunately, I got some offers and picked up a few small jobs, but nothing substantial. At least people were getting to know me, and folks in my business knew I was looking. I felt quite confident, especially because I knew I was better trained than my fellow tradesmen in the city. If it's true that in the land of the blind, a one-eyed man is king, then I had two eyes. It wouldn't be long before somebody needed a skilled mechanic like me.

Since neither of us had a steady job, we took the opportunity to get to know the city. We were fascinated by the Forte do Presépio, an old Portuguese fortress not far from other monuments, like the House with Eleven Windows, Santo Alexandre Church, and the Metropolitan Cathedral. Berta could have spent the whole day admiring those old buildings, rich with stories. Other favorite places of ours were the Praça da República, which is the setting of Belém's lovely theater, the Teatro da Paz, and the Bosque Rodrigues Alves, which is a slice of the wild Amazon forest right in the heart of downtown.

Our respite didn't last long, thank God. I was contacted by the owner of a body shop, Nicolau, who wanted to test me out on his own car, a 6-year-old Packard that had just been sitting there for lack of parts. "Now, there's a great way to get your car fixed for free and check out a new employee," I thought. Still, it was an interesting opportunity. I looked the vehicle over and found the trouble. Nothing serious. After I'd worked on the Packard for two days, it was back to running.

With the test complete, we settled on a contract. Nicolau would pay me by job, and I'd keep half of the labor charges. He'd also provide the tools and, if necessary, purchase replacement parts. I'd earn a small commission on parts too. Nicolau insisted we not sign a contract, because, as he said, our agreement had no expiration date; either side could rescind at any time. It wasn't a spectacular arrangement for me, but I finally had an income on which to rely, and we could rent a little house. Berta was overjoyed (period). We soon set about spinning plans for our future home.

We relied on the help of our new friends for the essentials, especially Moyses and Débora Bentes. We rented a house near them and bought a comfortable hammock to sleep in, an old stove, a makeshift table, and two chairs. Not bad considering we'd arrived only two weeks earlier. It's true I didn't have a steady job, but I made enough. My income covered our expenses just fine, and we even had a little left over. Wonderful!

Some days after we'd settled into our new home, it became clear that Berta was pregnant, as I'd begun to suspect. She was constantly nauseated and sleepy, her breasts had grown, and her period simply stopped coming. Our calculations left no doubt: the paradisiacal week we'd spent crossing the Mediterranean on the *MS Formosa* had yielded fruit. A baby!

Musing it over, I almost couldn't comprehend how much my life had changed. "I'm going to be a father, and the mother of our child is the most beautiful, tender woman in the world. We're getting along well in this new country and doing fine with the Portuguese language. I've got a job and even some new friends. Five months ago, I was a prisoner in a labor camp, with no future ahead of me and my very life in danger," I thought. Never in my wildest dreams could I have imagined that in such a short span of time I'd get married, travel halfway across the world, become a free man, a husband, a father – and be so happy. Life is full of surprises.

Two more Shabbat dinners and we'd learned even more about the Amazon. The Moroccan Jews had been important figures in the early settlement of the region,

but there were others who were even more important –
to start with, Native Americans belonging to dozens of
different tribes, along with their mestizo descendants,
known as "*caboclos.*" As waves of Portuguese and Spanish
immigrants arrived and conquered this giant territory, they
aligned themselves with the natives in order to survive
in a strange and hostile environment. In the loneliness of
the huge forest, many of the colonizers succumbed to the
charms of the sweet-scented, loving Indians and caboclas.
And thus began the great mixing of the races.

Moyses had transcribed a curious document issued
by the Portuguese Crown, which he had stumbled on while
looking through Pará's state archives. It was a Royal Decree,
published in Lisbon on April 4, 1755, by the Chancellery
General of the Court and Kingdom, and it showed how
the Crown and other Portuguese officials had considered
miscegenation an important challenge in the 18th century, a
matter of state in fact. One excerpt in particular caught my
attention: "And furthermore, the aforesaid subjects, who
have wed Indian women, as well as their descendants, shall
be designated by the name 'caboclos' or a similar term...
The same shall hold true for Portuguese women who wed
Indian men, and also for their children and descendants,
and to all I grant the same distinction."

The Africans who were brought as slaves to Brazil,
and to its rainforests, were part of this history as well.
Nearly 30,000 had landed at Amazon ports by 1788.

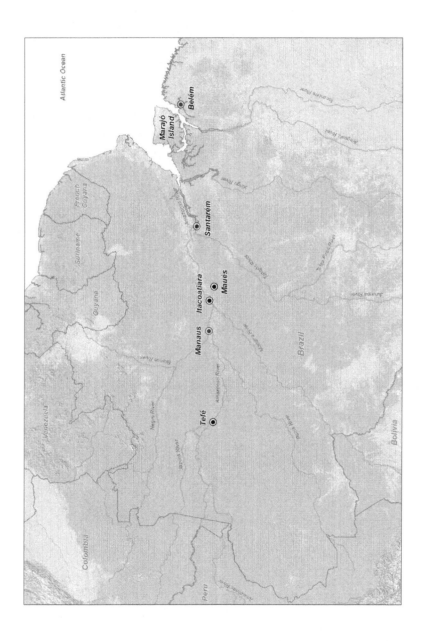

Following the Portuguese and the black Africans, close to half a million people had migrated from northeastern Brazil to the rainforest in the 19th century. Driven out by poverty and the endemic droughts that brutalize the region's arid backlands, these streams of humanity desperately sought to better their lives in the promising Amazon. It was rubber that brought the British, members of a powerful nation that boasted the world's most cutting-edge technology. Though there weren't many British immigrants, their numbers did not diminish their role. To them, the Amazon owes infrastructure that was advanced for its time in the realms of navigation, ports, electric power, running water and sewer, telegraphs, telephones, public lighting, trolleys, banks, and even tennis courts.

Syrian-Lebanese immigrants arrived as well, enriching the hues of an already colorful palette. Their reasons for coming were similar to those of the Jews, and they too imported their unique culture and family structure, plus a tremendous capacity for hard work. A few Americans also ventured down to the Amazon, drawn by the local need for more efficient transportation – railroads like the Madeira-Mamoré, ports, bridges, and, later, airports. The early 20th century saw the influx of the Japanese, who were not involved in rubber production but stuck solely to agriculture.

The process of migration was a complex one. Bachelors generally came first – Portuguese, Spanish, other Europeans, Northeasterners, Arabs, and Jews. They wasted no time spreading across the vast lands of the Amazon and finding ways to make a little money. Many of them would take native women and caboclas as concubines, have a lot of children with them, and only later send for a European woman from their own country, whom they would officially marry. The old racist adage from the days of Portuguese colonization was transplanted full force to the Amazon: a white woman for a wife, a mulatta for a lover, and a black woman for a servant. It is estimated that more than 200,000 descendants of Moroccan

Jews were living in the Amazon by 1942. Most were Catholics who preserved some of the habits of Jewish culture, though they themselves did not even know why – ergo, the colored stones you find next to tombs in Catholic cemeteries in remote corners of the Amazon, as well as the candles ablaze on Friday nights.

Portuguese, Spanish, and Arab immigrants left their traces in the settlements spread out along the mighty river. From 1850 to 1915, the participants in this mind-boggling process of miscegenation played a big part in the first Rubber Battle. Nearly three decades later, during World War II, when the vast majority of these new inhabitants were living in poverty, but in peaceful coexistence as well, the people of the Amazon forest were dragged into the second Rubber Battle, a government effort to rapidly and dramatically boost Brazilian rubber production, in part by encouraging the migration of Northeasterners to the Amazon. Oblivious to it all, Berta and I had landed in Brazil right in the middle of this second campaign.

* * * * *

"Gringos invade Germany!" I heard a newspaper vendor shout.

I dashed out of my office and bought a paper. The boy hadn't got it quite right. The Allies had actually invaded Normandy, in northern France. The mammoth battle hadn't reached German soil yet, but this undeniably marked the beginning of the end of the war in Europe. It was June 6, 1944 – D-Day.

Elated, I went to hunt down Moyses and share the joyous moment with him. I found the whole Bentes family gathered together. For them, the exciting news about the landing in Normandy was accompanied by word that Moyses' brother

Samuel had been drafted into the Brazilian Expeditionary Force. The troops had been deployed to Italy some time before, where 25,000 young Brazilians had engaged in bloody combat against the Axis forces. It was increasingly clear that England, the Soviet Union, the United States, and the other allies, including Brazil, were winning the war. Despite Germany's fierce resistance, it now seemed like ultimate victory was only a matter of time - and of thousands of lives, which continued to be wasted in the battlefields. The insanity was to continue for almost another year.

CHAPTER VIII

The Rubber Development Corporation

Berta's tummy was truly big now. She was still thin, but her belly…! I'd tease her, telling her that one day she'd fly through the air like a two-legged blimp. In all honesty, Berta was even more beautiful with her bulging belly, and I felt an incredible tenderness for that courageous woman who placed so much trust in me. We could already feel the new life developing inside her womb.

While Berta's belly was growing nonstop, I was working harder than ever. I'd been at Nicolau's garage for nearly two months when a decisive offer came along, one that suddenly changed our lives and helped to substantially increase my earnings. I was formally invited to sign on as an employee of the Rubber Development Corporation, then recently established to promote rubber production, enhance logistics in the Amazon, and improve transportation of this precious raw material to the U.S., where war efforts were being threatened by the possibility of an abrupt cutoff in supply. With Japan's surprise attack on Pearl Harbor, the Americans lost not only part of their Pacific fleet but also their main source of rubber: Malaysia's plantations. The situation was chaotic.

The stopgap solution was to reactivate the Amazon's natural rubber stands, which remained productive, albeit on a small scale. After the Vargas administration and the U.S. government signed the Washington Accords in 1942, the region enjoyed some relief from the economic devastation that had beleaguered it from 1915 until World War II. The agreements were aimed at rekindling and expanding the production of rubber, a raw material indispensable for any country at war.

This had very beneficial effects for the local economy, even though the commitments made by both governments held the price of rubber well below the expectations of Amazonian producers. The Washington Accords thus gave birth to the second Rubber Battle. Although shorter than the first, the second battle endowed the region with logistical infrastructure of enviable scope, all underwritten by generous funds from the United States.

One specific product of the second battle was the 1942 establishment of the Banco da Borracha – the Rubber Bank – which eventually became the Bank of the Amazon. In addition, the (U.S.) Rubber Reserve Company, later rechristened the Rubber Development Corporation, was responsible for setting up logistical support in the deep Amazon, among other places. It provided transportation and supplies. The pressing need for this raw material and the blockade of the Brazilian coast meant the company had to transport rubber from Manaus and Belém to Miami aboard Catalina and S-42 aircraft. Val-de-Cans Airport in Belém was thus revamped and expanded, and Ponta Pelada Airport was built in Manaus.

* * * * *

"Who's the boss around here?" I heard a male voice ask.

I crawled out from under a car to see two men, one short and dark and the other tall, thin, very white, and very blond.

The dark fellow was Brazilian, and the blond had to be a gringo.

The Brazilian man asked if I spoke English. I said I did, a little.

"Are you Mr. Hazan?" the blond inquired in his native tongue.

"Yes, that's me," I replied, using what little English I spoke.

Of the languages I knew, English was arguably my weakest. I could manage to read and understand it quite well, but when it came to speaking, I didn't feel comfortable.

"Can we sit somewhere and talk? I'm Garry Smith, better known around here as Cowboy."

I offered him a chair, but Smith turned it down, preferring to stand. "Not now," he said. "We need more time; it'll be a long conversation. How about tonight? It's a matter of your interest. Give me your address, and I'll have a car fetch you."

I told him where I lived, and he said he'd arrange for me to be picked up at 6 o'clock that evening at my home. The dark fellow, who must have been his interpreter, barely took part in the conversation. My English seemed to be doing the job.

At 6 sharp, a jeep pulled up in front of our house, and I said goodbye to Berta – who was dying of curiosity – and went off to meet Cowboy. I soon realized we were headed for the recently reopened Val-de-Cans Airport.

After inviting me to sit down to dinner with him, Smith cut to the chase: the Americans needed a mechanic to take care of the maintenance of planes belonging to Pan American and the Brazilian carrier Panair, which were landing in Belém daily.

"But I don't know anything about aircraft," I tried to argue.

"To judge from the information I've been given, you're a good car mechanic, maybe the best in Belém. That's a good start," Smith countered. "You'll have a set salary and be a registered employee of the Rubber Development Corporation. I'm the head mechanic now, and I intend to train you for a few months until you get to be a skilled tradesman and can take over the whole operation."

The salary was several times what I was earning. Besides making more money, I'd receive quality training, something hard to come by in those days, and that could serve as a springboard for other opportunities. I said yes but asked if my inadequate English would present a problem.

"No, because you understand a lot," said my new boss, "and you can express yourself reasonably well. Not many folks in Brazil can communicate in English. And that's even truer in Belém." We shook hands.

I gave a little prayer of thanks that I had read so many books and newspapers in English, both in Istanbul and while on board the *Jamaïque*. All that reading contributed to my knowledge of the language. Much sooner than I could have imagined, I'd be reaping the fruits of my labor.

It was quite late when I got home, but Berta was lying in the hammock, wide awake, anxiously waiting for me. I told her the news, and I could tell she was excited. I saw the tears she tried to hide in vain. Because of her pregnancy, she'd been very sensitive lately, be it good news or bad.

"We'll have to buy a crib and maybe find a girl who can help me right after the birth, Mr. Hazan," she said as she snuggled into my arms. I felt like the most powerful man in the world.

"Mrs. Hazan, tomorrow we'll go out and find the most beautiful crib in all Belém. We also have to buy a real bed for us. Sleeping in a hammock might be nice for a few days, but enough already! You're going to need more comfort in the next few months. And I think Moyses and Débora can help us find a maid. I'll tell Nicolau the news first thing in the morning, and over the next week or so, I'll finish all the repairs I've started on," I explained, a bit anxious myself. "Everything is falling into place, thank goodness."

"I'm so proud of you," Berta said, and she fell asleep in my arms, a little smile on her lips.

In the subsequent months, Smith proved to be an excellent teacher, and I was an applied and dedicated student. Whenever I had a little time on my hands, I'd read maintenance manuals in English and speak English, both with the American pilots who landed almost every day and with the Rubber Development Corporation's locally engaged staff. My English improved by leaps and bounds, and soon I had no trouble communicating.

I also tried to keep abreast of the latest news, and so early on September 9, 1944, I learned that the Red Army had crossed the Danube and occupied Bulgaria. My heart quickened. It was over! The nightmare had ended, and the next step was to urgently find David, Salvator, and all my other friends. I asked Cowboy for permission to leave early and hurried home.

"Berta!" I shouted from the doorway. "Our Bulgaria is free again!"

Berta came running into my arms. "I knew it would happen soon. It's so wonderful to hear that it's true at last!" she cried.

"We've got to write our friends and relatives now. Nobody has a clue where we are," I added.

We spent the day writing letters. I sent one to my old address in Sofia, where I expected David to go now that Bulgaria was no longer under German rule. I also wrote to Salvator Mairoff's parents, asking them for news about my dear friend. I mailed another letter to Nissim Michael, Berta's cousin and my friend. We'd gotten his address in Madrid from Mr. Farhi when we were in Istanbul. Meanwhile, Berta wrote to the Gerassi family, asking for news about Rachamim and his wife, Estreja. We were worried, because they were advancing in age. We remembered Omer as well, in far-off Istanbul, and sent him a postcard of Belém.

The next weeks were filled with eager anticipation as we waited for answers from Bulgaria and, more importantly, for the arrival of our first child. Berta coped with her enormous belly – as everything else – with contagious fortitude. She was radiantly happy. We'd already picked out names. If it was a boy, he'd be called Daniel, after my father, and if it was a girl, Sara, after Berta's mother and also after Queen Sarah-Theodora, Bulgaria's 14th-century Jewish monarch who converted to Christianity.

Before we had heard anything from Bulgaria, we received a letter from Leon Farhi in reply to our brief missive about our move to Brazil. I've hung on to many of the letters I thought were important from back then, along with copies of our replies.

Dear Berta and Licco,

I'm very happy that we're in contact once again. I was really quite worried by the lack of news.

I don't know much about Brazil, but I imagine it's a country filled with opportunities for a young, well-educated couple like yourselves.

Do be careful, though, because tropical climates harbor dangers like malaria, leprosy, and other diseases that are strange to us Europeans. My children, Saul and Eva, have also been following your journey, first in Turkey and now in Brazil, and they wish you every success. Keep me abreast of everything that happens to you.

Warmest regards from your friend,
Leon

I wrote back the very same day:

Belém
September 27, 1944

Dear Mr. Farhi,

As always, I was very happy to receive your letter. We are adapting to Brazil. We live in Belém, a city on the mouth of the Amazon River in the far north of the country, almost on the equator. Yesterday our son, Daniel, was born, a healthy baby who loves to cry. Berta is still quite weak, but that is offset by our great happiness.

I've got a job as a mechanic at the Belém airport. I work for an American company called the Rubber Development Corporation, and my salary is quite reasonable. I'm learning how to repair planes instead of cars, and I'm doing well at it.

Big changes have occurred in Bulgaria in recent months. As you must be aware, the Russians drove out the Germans, and the country joined the Allies in the war against Germany – a tad late, admittedly. I don't know what the new government's politics are, but all indications are that you'll soon have your companies back. If you need my help to regain control of American Car or to resolve any other matter, I am always at your service. I hope justice will be done. Given how brief my stay at American Car was, it would be more than fair for me to return all of the stock that is officially in my name to your family. How should I go about doing that?

I haven't been able to get in contact with my brother, David, yet, but I do hope to hear from him and receive news from Bulgaria soon. I've written several letters to friends and family, and I'm confident that I'll hear back from them shortly. Thank God the war will soon be over.

ILKO MINEV

Berta and I would like to wish you and your family all the best. We look forward to hearing from you again. We will always be grateful for everything you've done for us.

Berta and Licco Hazan

It was a while before any replies came from Bulgaria. When we finally did hear from people, the news was at times uplifting and at other times very sad. David was the first to reply, with a laconic letter. He was fine but very busy because of the responsibilities he'd taken on with the Patriotic Front, which held power in Bulgaria. It appeared that my brother, as a veteran of the resistance, was influential, respected, and full of optimism. I could breathe a sigh of relief.

Then we got word that Salvator had passed away a few weeks after I left the labor camp. I was devastated for days on end. His merry laughter kept ringing in my ears, and I could almost feel him next to me. But then the cold, hard reality would hit me again: my friend was dead. Berta, who only knew Salvator from my stories, joined me in my pain and tears. "He was the happiest, most decent, delightful human being I've ever known. He loved me so much. And I loved him!" I voiced my thoughts aloud. "No one deserves to die just months before liberation. Especially not Salvator."

Our suffering was only lessened by our little Daniel. Once he got over his initial colic, he proved to be a very sweet, quiet baby. He had Berta's dimples and her easygoing nature. Fearing possible complications, we were nervous on the day of his *brit milah* – the Jewish circumcision ceremony – but we heard nothing save a tiny whimper from him during the procedure, and off he went to sleep. He woke up whiny later, crying for the breast. We were smitten. That little piece of life that depended on us was the most important thing in the world for Berta and me, two inexperienced rookies.

Daniel was barely over a month old when Garry, the Cowboy, said he wanted to have another important talk with me. We got together for lunch, and, as always, he went straight to the point: "Licco, I think your apprenticeship is over. I don't have much left to teach you, and I've got to admit that training you was much easier than I'd imagined. Now Rubber Development needs you as its head mechanic, but in Manaus. You'll get a substantial raise, the company will pay for your move, and it'll also cover the rent on your new place for a year. It's a three-year contract. You can be called an expert now, and you're going to earn like one."

"But, boss, my son was just born. I rented a house not long ago with a two-year lease. And anyway, I've got to talk this over with Berta. We've got attachments here, friends, a maid. I don't know if she'll be interested."

Garry grinned. "From what I know of your wife, she's going to say yes. She's a brave, determined woman, and she knows what she wants. Nobody's got a better head for numbers, and she'll be quick to figure out that this is a very fine offer. You're a lucky man to have married a woman like her." Garry was certain it was an excellent opportunity, and he wanted to convince me. "Just think, you'll be employed by the U.S. government, and you'll have a very well-paying job with a renewable three-year contract. Your current contract is only good for a year, much of which has already elapsed. If there's a penalty for breaking your lease, Rubber Development will cover your losses. What more could you ask for?"

Cowboy did indeed know Berta well. In fact, she was friends with his girlfriend, Maria, an attractive cabocla with broad hips and a generous bust, qualities that were typically appreciated by gringos like Garry. She didn't have much schooling, but she was smart, happy, and outgoing, and Berta had quickly taken a liking to her.

My young wife found the proposal very attractive. She

was without question courageous, ready to take on anything, and amazingly practical. We talked it over with Moyses and Débora Bentes before we all agreed that the proposed terms were excellent. Even though we were sad to be leaving our friends, we felt the challenge would be worthwhile.

Before we left Belém, Garry and Maria got married. After the war, they resettled, in the United States, in Louisiana. When we next saw them, in 1958, they had three children. Maria's English was still quite shaky, yet her Portuguese had also gone downhill, leaving her with heavy accents in both languages. It was actually comical. Luckily enough, Cowboy found it all quite charming. During our reunion, we had great fun reminiscing about the good old days in Belém. Garry always joked that he'd trained me to be an expert mechanic. An expert, according to him, was someone who knew a lot about a little, until he became someone who knew everything about nothing. Prior to my apprenticeship, I had been a jack of all trades, one of those who knew a little about a lot. Garry liked to joke that once I achieved perfection, I would know nothing about everything.

Up until a few years ago, we always got entertaining Christmas letters from Garry, who, like Maria, is no longer with us. That's the trouble with growing old: you lose something or someone important every day. And yet there are folks who have the gall to call these our golden years. Nonsense!

We scheduled our trip to Manaus on a ship from the renowned Booth Line, a partner of Rubber Development. The two businesses were involved in a number of ventures together. The Booth Line hauled a lot of cargo back and forth from Manaus to Belém, and we relied quite heavily on their services. So the captain arranged a special cabin for us, extremely comfortable and spacious.

After our experience on the *Jamaïque*, we thought we were in paradise. It was a cargo ship, and we were the sole passengers. We soon made friends with the captain, who pointed out the highlights along the way. Over the course of our seven-day journey, we finally came to understand the true dimensions of the Amazon. We felt the force of the mighty river and admired the immense rainforest.

The Breves Narrows was breathtaking. There, the Amazon River suddenly tapers to a stream, and the current intensifies as an enormous volume of water squeezes through a very tight space. The captain told us the river must be at least a hundred meters deep there. A frightening thought, actually! The large and lovely Xingu, Madeira, and Tapajós Rivers flow into the main channel, and you witness a spectacular new display each time this occurs. Each river is different, but they all share a wild beauty, fearsome yet enticing. For example, in contrast with the muddy Amazon, the clear green waters of the beautiful Tapajós River flow between beaches of fine white sand. The small town of Santarém stands on its banks, completely cut off from the rest of the world.

"If there's a heaven on earth, it must be somewhere around here. Some day we'll return, and we can luxuriate in this beauty," I whispered in Berta's ear.

Our arrival in Manaus was glorious. The city is located on the left bank of the majestic Negro River, with its clean dark waters. And it has a floating dock. Its riverbanks are lined with charming buildings from the time of the British. The first sight that greets you is the dramatic meeting of the rapid and muddy waters of the yellowish Solimões with the dark waters of the Negro. These two giants flow side by side for a while, never mixing, as they set about forming the Amazon, which discharges the largest volume of water in the world. It's an extraordinary place! From the confluence of the waters onward, we watched freshwater dolphins escort our ship to the port of Manaus.

"Licco, I love it! I think this could be our land, and we

could build our home here," Berta said, glowing. Precisely what I was thinking at that very moment.

"Manaus was a big village when I came on scene, and I turned it into a modern city." In 1896, this sentence was pronounced by Governor Eduardo Gonçalves Ribeiro at the end of his second term of office. Although there's a lot of truth to his words, one thing is certain: as a good politician often does, the governor was putting all modesty aside. After Ribeiro and the astounding prosperity of the bygone rubber era, the city fell into a steady decline.

When we moved to Manaus in early 1945, it was a quiet little town of about 100,000, while the population of the state of Amazonas was nearly 500,000. Like Belém, it was apparent that the city had known better days in the not-too-distant past. Built during the height of the rubber boom, stately Portuguese mansions with high, thick walls and huge windows that allow for sufficient air circulation were a salient feature of the cityscape.

Only the downtown streets were paved and tree-lined. The city's infrastructure functioned well, but it had decayed somewhat in comparison to what the British had bequeathed it in the early 20th century. The main difference between then and now was that now there was hardly any electrical lighting anywhere in Manaus. Since power generation was unreliable and fell short of demand, priority was given to supplying educational institutions, like the law school, as well as key public agencies and some of the teachers' houses. One alternative was to install your own electrical generator, but few could afford it because the purchase price was so steep and the maintenance fees exorbitant.

Life in Manaus was far from easy, with many young folks leaving to study in the large cities of southern Brazil. Educational and job options were few and far between. There weren't spots for many students at the town's only college, and in any case the school offered more of a disincentive for students looking for solid learning and a brighter future. Virtually all goods and job opportunities were scarce. It was a very tough period for everyone. A black market was inevitable since all food was rationed. A good number of people made money by obtaining quotas from government agencies and selling them to those in true need.

Finding a place to rent in a city in such a state of decline was easy enough, as we soon chose a large house on Joaquim Nabuco Avenue, situated downtown. We'd be living in close proximity to some magnificent sites, like the port of Manaus and its floating dock, the Teatro Amazonas opera house, the Palace of Justice, the Customs House, the busy Mercado Municipal marketplace, some of the town's main churches, and Clube Ideal, a social club for the well-to-do. We were very well situated, in the heart of these reminders of a glorious past. We didn't even need the tram, which ran solely on those rare occasions when there was power.

During the war, there was a curious system for circulating the top news stories around Manaus. Not very many folks had radios, so a shrieking siren advised downtown residents whenever something major happened. People would rush to Eduardo Ribeiro Avenue and crowd around the front of the *Jornal do Comércio* newspaper office, where the latest news would be written on a huge blackboard. It wasn't the most modern means of communication, but it worked.

The local economy had been revitalized by the second Rubber Battle, but not robustly enough. And masses of Northeastern migrants continued to pour in, along with a few adventurers from other parts of Brazil. It seemed like the city wanted to rise again.

Ponta Pelada Airport was a good distance from downtown, but whenever I needed, a Rubber Development jeep would pick me up at home and drop me off at the end of my workday. Back then, Panair and Pan American often used hydroplanes on the route to Manaus, and they would land right alongside the port, not far from my house. Most of the time, I'd be at the floating pier, where the planes docked and where there was a repair shop and small office. When more space was needed later, the floating dock was transferred to the neighborhood of Educandos, where riverboat traffic wasn't as heavy. The hydroplanes usually took off early, and so I'd work nights and into the morning hours. There were only six non-American employees at Rubber Development Corporation in Manaus, and we were always treated very nicely. In those days, it was a privilege to be hired by the company, which paid well and on time.

Before we left Belém, Moyses Bentes had given me the names of several friends of his who lived in Manaus. He'd lived there himself for a while and knew a lot of folks. After we had a few days to settle in, we decided to look up some of Moyses' acquaintances. The synagogue was always a good place to start.

Rebby Meyr Synagogue stood on Praça 15 de Novembro, a public square not far from our home. The first person we spotted there was a striking, short fellow, whose stature was typical of a Moroccan Jew. The fact that he was missing a chunk of his left ear was quite noticeable, and he made no attempt to hide it. Since we arrived quite early and there wasn't a *minyan* yet, he and I had a quick chat.

"I'm Jacob Azulay, the congregation's *sheliah*. Are you Jewish too?" he asked in Portuguese with a heavy Moroccan accent.

I summed up our journey so far, and Jacob responded with a bit of history about the Jewish community in Manaus.

A large number of the Jews in Manaus – almost all of Moroccan heritage – came from the interior of the Amazon or from Belém. Bankrupt and broken by the rubber crash, many of them had resettled in Manaus around 1930, where they joined the community already living there. Most were from Itacoatiara, Parintins, Maués, and other small towns that had thrived during the rubber boom and then been ruined by its collapse.

Unfortunately, we only had time to exchange superficial information before more people arrived and the service began. Family names in Manaus and Belém were much the same, attesting to common roots. I asked about Elias Benzecry, a friend of Moyses Bentes, and was told that he attended a different synagogue, Beth Ya'acov, on Ramos Ferreira Street, the former Praça da Saudade. Just like in Belém, grumpy old men had quarreled and consequently divided what had already been small enough to start with.

The next week, we went to the other synagogue, where we met Elias, an athletically built gentleman with a constant smile and shrill voice, who kindly invited me to sit with his family and friends. Outsiders weren't common in Manaus, and, like in Belém, everybody wanted to meet the newcomers. That day, I was introduced to many members of the Sabbá, Benzecry, Benchimol, Israel, Benoliel, Laredo, and Assayag families, among others. Much to our happiness, and to the congregation's good fortune, the two improvised synagogues in Manaus merged in 1962 and built a new temple called Beth Yaacov/Rebi Meyr.

We couldn't have asked for a warmer welcome in Manaus, and I soon felt at home. I had no clue I was meeting people who would be with me for the rest of my life. Echoing our experience in Belém, it soon became clear that it wouldn't be hard to forge friendships in Manaus. Berta, too, made friends in the community.

In the months that followed, we met a lot of people, both inside the Jewish community and out. In Bulgaria's fine liberal style, Berta and I always sought to diversify our friendships and never embraced the notion of voluntary segregation that some people impose for religious or ethnic reasons. We wanted to have friends of all beliefs and colors, like the Brazilians, so brilliantly described by Stefan Zweig.

My job allowed me to devote part of my time to other activities, and so I would fix cars that weren't running for lack of parts. I became well known in the city, and we were invited to join the Bosque Clube, where Manaus's elite spent their weekends. For us, this was an important social conquest. Our passion for tennis began there and remained with us for the rest of our lives. At 82, I could still tackle a game of doubles, and even though I could barely move, I did manage to get the ball over the net. That's not possible anymore, and today my love of tennis is confined to watching the Grand Slams on TV and admiring players like Roger Federer and Rafael Nadal.

After a few months, we were already part of the festive Amazon society. Daniel was growing and turning into a healthy, happy child. He was already standing a lot, and it wouldn't be long before he'd be walking. Everything seemed to be going our way. We thought we'd finally found our place in the sun.

And quite literally, we did! Manaus is hot and humid, with the thermometer never dropping below 68 nor climbing above 100. But the humidity skyrockets to 90 percent in the rainy season, when vertical rivers of water come gushing down. It actually didn't take us long to get used to the climate, and we even came to find it pleasant. Although our everyday lives were rather uneventful, we found plenty of small reasons for happiness. We spent our Sundays strolling along Eduardo Ribeiro Avenue, watching movies at the Cine Avenida, and eating ice cream at the Leiteria Amazonas or Bar Americano. When we had the energy, we'd hop a tram on the Saudade or Remédios lines.

When the river was at its lowest level, a cornucopia of foodstuffs could be bought at the Mercado Municipal, especially fish, which came in all types and sizes. It's a shame that the months of low water are short-lived, because that's when the locals can plant in the fertile land bordering the river, yielding an abundance of produce. The waters begin rising in December and during some years can reach an amazing 50 feet – yet another extravagant feature of the Amazon.

While all this was going on, we received regular letters from Bulgaria, updating us from afar on the lives of my brother and our friends and acquaintances. Rachamim and Estreja Gerassi had made it to Palestine – God only knows how – and were living in Tel Aviv. We also managed to locate my friend and Berta's cousin, Nissim Michael, and soon heard from him. He was doing very well in Madrid and had been given authorization to distribute a revolutionary new medicine in Spain: Streptomycin, an antibiotic that had been discovered in the laboratory of Dr. Selman Abraham Waksman. By a quirk of fate, Nissim had had the opportunity to meet the doctor, and they'd become friends. Nissim was over the moon, because Streptomycin was the first drug that could cure tuberculosis and demand for it promised to be huge. Years later, Madrid honored Dr. Waksman by naming a street after him. A well-deserved tribute.

Though the war dragged on, the end did seem to draw ever closer. There was no doubt who the winners and losers would be. Meanwhile, survivors were turning up in various corners, looking to start new lives.

In early May 1945, the war ended in Europe. When the news broke, Moyses Bentes' brother, Samuel, was at the port of Santos, where he was supposed to ship out to Italy after lengthy training with the Brazilian Expeditionary Force. His suitcase did head off to the front, along with other supplies, but he managed to disembark in time. And so the brave soldier, Samuel, won the war and finished his military career without taking part in a single battle.

The details reached us some days later. After bloody fighting, the Russians had taken eastern Berlin, while the

Americans and British had invaded from the west. They found a skeleton of a city. Trapped in his bunker, Hitler killed himself, and Germany surrendered. We followed the news from Europe in shock: towns in ruins, and hardship, hunger, and death all around. The world finally realized the true dimensions of the atrocities and barbaric acts committed during those dark years, which we now know as the Holocaust.

Names we'd never heard of – like Dachau, Buchenwald, Auschwitz, Bergen-Belsen, Treblinka, Theresienstadt, and so many others – appeared over and again in the news and soon were emblems of the abominations that had been perpetrated, and in the 20th century no less. Tens of millions had been killed. The war had destroyed the lives of soldiers and civilians alike. We could be grateful that we had survived a tragedy unmatched by any the world had ever witnessed.

Once the celebrating was over, life returned to normal – a life that wasn't at all easy for most residents in Manaus. The local economy couldn't sustain the residents, let alone those who continued to flow in from the northeast and other parts of Brazil, where things were even worse. Thanks to the security of my contract with Rubber Development, Berta and I had no immediate worries, but we were undoubtedly a glaring exception to the rule.

* * * * *

One day, noticing that Berta had grown restless, I said, "Spit it out! What's on your mind now?"

"Licco, the war is going to end in the Pacific too. This job of yours is great, but it might be gone soon. We need to think about something else."

"My contract is good for three years, so we don't really need to worry yet. But, as always, you're right." I had to agree with Berta. "We can't leave it for the last minute. We've got to look for other possibilities for when this blessed contract runs out. I suppose our first measure should be to tighten our belts and put aside a little nest egg, don't you think?"

"The economy in Manaus is in a real slump, but I've seen how some people have managed to rise above it – through lots of hard work and creativity," Berta replied. "It's true. You know that fellow, Isaac Sabbá, who dreams of building a refinery here? He's a small man, but he certainly thinks big. That must be why he's one of the few people who have been successful."

I had to agree yet again. We decided we'd start thinking about our own business. It probably wouldn't be a refinery, but it could very well be a body shop. In the early days of peacetime, there would continue to be a need for aircraft technicians in Manaus, of that I was certain, and this meant we'd still be in a comfortable position. Yet it was worth checking out alternatives.

On August 6, 1945, the news came that the U.S. had dropped a historically unprecedented type of bomb on the city of Hiroshima. The Japanese, however, would not give an inch, and as the final battle edged ever closer to them, they engaged in a bloody conflict where thousands of soldiers and many civilians lost their lives. The Japanese commanders and the Imperial House refused to accept imminent defeat and ignored the warnings of the Allies, who had threatened to take drastic action. The Little Boy bomb had been a cruel confirmation of these threats.

Just three days later, on August 9, 1945, the U.S. launched its second nuclear attack, this time striking Nagasaki with an even larger bomb, dubbed Fat Man. In the midst of chaos and civilian panic, Japan's military was forced to its knees and had to recognize defeat.

On August 16, Emperor Hirohito ordered Japanese troops to halt their fighting. The cannons were silenced, and a hard-won peace ushered in a new post-war world (imperfect, true, but considerably better). And thus, the war was over at last. One of the new peace's ramifications was felt in the region where we lived: the U.S. resumed its regular imports of rubber from Southeast Asia – where it was cheaper than in Brazil – and Brazil's second Rubber Battle likewise met its demise. In the midst of celebrating the end of World War II, the Amazon saw its economic foundation collapse. The Rubber Development Corporation no longer served any purpose. Berta had been on target once again.

It was amazing how quickly we felt the impact of events on the other side of the world. Brazil's rubber industry no longer had anyone to sell to, and since rubber represented the region's main economic activity, the local economy was hit hard. This triggered a disorderly exodus from the interior to urban centers like Belém and Manaus, leading to substandard urbanization and a chaotic concentration of people. The outcomes of this process are notorious: bloated cities and the demographic draining of the interior. These problems have only worsened and now, in the early 21st century, continue to await some kind of solution.

All non-American employees at the Rubber Development Corporation were laid off and given severance packages. With my contract still in effect, I stayed on and was put in charge of settling all outstanding business. When those jobs were finished, Cowboy Garry Smith came to Manaus, along with another American whose name I've forgotten. They were assigned to terminate all operations under the Washington Accords. They had just closed down the company's operations in Belém, and now it was Manaus's turn.

Under the Brazil-U.S. agreement, the Americans held 40 percent of the Banco da Borracha. They ceded this stock to the Brazilian government, who used it to found the Banco da Amazônia S.A., which continues to play a vital role in regional development. The Rubber Development Corporation, however, was not as lucky; it was dismantled. Since I had two and a half years left on my contract, we had to reach an agreement. Negotiations were quick and easy thanks to the assistance of my friend Garry. I got to keep the company jeep and all the tools used to repair aircraft. I also received a lump-sum settlement equivalent to two years in wages. For my part, I agreed to help solve any problem or pending issue that might arise over the course of the next few years.

I must admit it was an excellent agreement, one that positioned me to open my own business. Since I had a fair amount of capital and the time to better evaluate any opportunities, I could afford to make decisions carefully. I continued to be well paid for servicing the Panair aircraft that connected Manaus to the rest of the world. The only real difference was that I no longer had a fixed contract or was compensated by Rubber Development. Instead, the airline paid me directly.

Berta and I were able to open a body shop that guaranteed us a steady stream of income, before we risked aiming any higher. The shop, which we named Berimex in honor of Berta, didn't require large investments since I had inherited a sizable collection of modern tools from Rubber Development. At the same time, since there was ample space in the huge house on Instalação Street, which we leased for the shop, Berta started working as a parts distributor for diesel engines, a service that was unavailable in Manaus. It proved to be a wise business choice, because so many diesel boats were needed to transport cargo and passengers to towns deep in the Amazon wilderness.

Our next step was to hire Gustavo, a young mechanic I liked very much, who had worked with me at Ponta Pelada Airport. He was jobless and jumped at the offer. Years later, this decision was validated as the best I could have made. In 1954, Gustavo became a partner at the shop, and, in 1973, he further increased his participation by buying a good share of my stock in the company. Grounded in years of mutual respect and admiration, this story of business success hasn't come to an end. Together with my son, Daniel, who is the current company president, Gustavo's sons manage Berimex, now one of the largest car and truck dealerships in northern Brazil. Under Daniel's management, the company has grown substantially and built a solid reputation. I still own some shares, more for sentimental than financial reasons. I want to hold on to my memories of building this business, which I did with so much love and devotion.

CHAPTER IX

The world turns

Tempus regit actum
(Time rules the act)

The news out of Bulgaria wasn't very encouraging. The communists had taken over the Patriotic Front, and the country was galloping toward a totalitarian regime, which the communists themselves called the "dictatorship of the proletariat." From the eyewitness reports of friends who had emigrated in time, we learned that the regime was increasingly adopting Soviet methods and standards. All assets had been expropriated, there was total censorship, and the Communist Party controlled all means of communication. They ruled everyone's life with an iron fist and wielded power over everything. Sycophants and otherwise unqualified people rose to vital posts, and any display of dissatisfaction or protest was labeled treason and subject to punishment.

The Communist Party was considered infallible, and its top leader in every country, the Secretary-General, was treated as a god. This is how it went in Bulgaria, Romania, Poland, Hungary, East Germany, Mongolia, Korea, China, and, many years later, in Cuba. As to be expected, the supreme god, to whom everyone else had to report, resided in Moscow. Dancing to the tune of the USSR, Bulgaria had now created its own Gulag, which was the destination of those who were dissatisfied, who had been defamed, or who had been denounced for some act of disloyalty.

So far, none of this had had a direct impact on my brother, David, thank God. He had even been sent to Moscow on a full scholarship to study industrial chemistry. David had been an active participant in the resistance against the fascists, and he'd probably brandished a weapon or two fighting alongside some of the new leaders. All indications were that he was being groomed to occupy major posts in the new regime.

I also received news from Farhi. He told me that not only were his companies not returned to him but also that the people's militia had gone after him at his old address in Sofia, attempting to arrest him as a capitalist and thus an exploiter of the people. The militia was actually a cruel police force that the people had nothing to do with and one that committed all sorts of atrocities. Petrov, our former accountant, said they had come after me as well, because they thought that I represented some threat to the dictatorship of the proletariat as the former owner of American Car. I was worried and wrote David. His reply came two months later, explaining that it was understandable that some things would get out of hand at the outset of the new regime, but that it would all be cleared up in short order. The future of Bulgaria and its brother countries in the communist bloc would prove the superiority of the communist system over bourgeois capitalism. It was just a matter of time, David insisted.

A few days after I received my brother's letter, I got another, this one from my friend Nissim Michael in Spain. Its contents were worrisome and volatile.

Madrid
June 28, 1946

Dear Licco,

I'm sorry it's taken so long for me to reply to your letter. I have a serious problem and urgently need your help. I've been arrested here in Madrid because of my false documents, which state that I'm a German officer. I got these papers from Mr. Denev, the Skoda employee in Sofia, who in turn got them from Mr. Albert Göring. Since I speak German and I'm fair-skinned and blond, it wasn't hard to fool the guards at the Sofia airport. Right in the middle of the war, I flew from Sofia to Rome by military plane and then took another plane from Rome to Madrid. Since I had no other choice, I kept on using the German documents until three months ago, when I was arrested by British intelligence. They think I'm a German fugitive, a war criminal from the SS, Gestapo, or something like that. At first, I was held incommunicado. Now, at least I've been allowed to write and receive letters.

I hope you'll be able to help me prove that I'm really who I am: a Bulgarian Jew, that is. I tried to explain everything to a British investigator, but he thought the story was so incredible that he didn't believe a single word. To make things worse, my case has been pushed to the back of the line, and now there are at least 300 some ahead of me. Of course I'll prove my innocence eventually and be freed, but without your help, that might take several months. I believe your testimony will set the record straight and can resolve my problem quickly. Because of the communist regime, I can't count on assistance from Bulgaria. I'm also appealing to Mr. Leon Farhi, who helped me escape and is quite familiar with my story.

Someone else who suffered false imprisonment a good while ago in Germany, along with the Nazi leaders, is Mr. Albert Göring, to whom we all owe so much. I believe that you, Farhi, and I can also provide testimony on his behalf.

Warmest regards from your friend, who is rotting away in prison, this time a victim of friendly fire,

Nissim

I knew it would take a long time for a letter to get to him from Manaus, so I telegraphed Leon Farhi with the news. I didn't have the slightest idea how to proceed and I needed his advice once again. Luckily, he got right back to me, by telegram as well. I've still got his message:

Nissim free. Albert not yet. Measures taken. No help needed now.

I breathed a sigh of relief. Berta read and reread the telegram and then broke down sobbing. I held her in my arms and tried to comfort her.

"Baruch Hashem! Blessed be the name of the Lord!" she whispered. "This damned war! It won't leave us alone."

That very next instant, Daniel picked himself up off the floor on shaky legs and took his first steps. We stopped and stared at him in a daze for a few seconds, (comma) and then Berta's tears blended with a euphoric smile.

Almost a month later, we received another letter from Nissim, which explained everything. His first letter had taken nearly two months to reach Manaus. In the meantime, the daughter of the British ambassador had contracted a very serious illness, and the doctors had prescribed high doses of Streptomycin. Since the drug was new then, it wasn't easy to acquire, not even when the patient was the British ambassador's daughter. In the midst of this despair, someone thought of Nissim, who had been working with the antibiotic prior to his arrest. The outcome was predictable: with Nissim's decisive help, the young girl was saved. Nissim Michael's case went straight to processing, and he was set free.

After his release, Nissim testified on behalf of Albert Göring. Many other people, including Leon Farhi, had done the same, (comma) and now he just had to be freed. Despite the hefty evidence in his favor, however, it took a year for that to happen. Later, he was arrested again before being released some months later. His accursed last name followed him relentlessly to the end of his days, with his humanitarian acts never duly recognized during his lifetime. Yet we are all indebted to that extraordinary man.

* * * * *

Daniel had turned 2 when we began suspecting that Berta might be pregnant again. Perhaps it wasn't the best timing, because she was working hard at Berimex. Our business with diesel engine parts was going strong, and other opportunities were appearing. My beautiful wife was a talented businesswoman, while she was also my best friend, and on top of that, a most dedicated mother. Despite our busy lives, it would be really nice to have a little brother or sister for Daniel, we told ourselves with a sigh of joy.

Much to my chagrin, my brother, David, very rarely wrote. He was still in Moscow, where he would spend another two years. I thought his letters were a tad dry and didn't contain much information, but all signs were that he was happy and healthy. I wrote him about the impending arrival of our second child and told him a bit about our new life in Manaus. To my wonder, David wrote back saying that he too was expecting a child, in March of the next year. He'd met Irina, a beautiful Russian classmate, at the university. One thing had led to another, (comma) and they'd fallen in love. Now she was pregnant, and they were going to get married soon. I didn't need to worry, he assured me, because they both had scholarships and wouldn't be in any financial bind.

By the time I received his next letter, they were already married. So I did the only thing I could and sent them a congratulatory telegram. There are so few of us Jews in the world that I always think it's a shame when one of us marries outside the faith. According to our religion, it's the mother who defines whether descendants are Jewish or not; it's not enough for the father to be Jewish. This meant David's children wouldn't be, so they wouldn't be part of our long history and our traditions stretching back over 5,000 years. But all of that was secondary right then, and the most important thing was my only brother's happiness. Sara, our daughter, and Oleg, David's son, were born in March 1948, separated by a difference of just a few days but many, many miles.

Sara's birth didn't alter our lives much. It's true that I did spend even more time working, but our routine went unchanged. The good news was that we could afford a kerosene refrigerator, which made Berta's life much easier. The next step was to purchase an electric generator, admittedly quite expensive, but well worth it. We kept the device running from 6 to 9 at night, and that gave me extra time with the children. Daniel was demanding more attention, and since Berta was busy with Sara, I needed to lend a hand.

As soon as Sara was a bit bigger, we resumed spending our leisure hours at the Bosque Clube, where the children had a lot of fun. Our other favorite pastime was to visit friends who had a "*banho*." That was what the locals called a weekend home with a paradisiacal brook of cold, crystal-clear water running through it. Although most *banhos* weren't far from town, they were hard to get to, because there were absolutely no paved roads. We still had our blessed jeep, inherited from Rubber Development, so the makeshift dirt roads weren't a big problem for us. The children loved these places; on hot Manaus days, they offered matchless respite. It's a shame – the same brooks that were a source of such delight back then are the very same streams of filthy, stinky water that crisscross the metropolis of Manaus today.

After getting his degree in chemistry, David returned to Sofia, where he held one of the top posts in Bulgaria's hierarchy of technocrats. He was a member of the Communist Party, of course, and a loyal follower of Stalinist, Leninist, and Marxist dogma. This bothered me a great deal, because alarming news was leaking from the Soviet Union and other countries, including Bulgaria. Only a short time before, Stalin, Beria, and accomplices had promoted purges within both the party and the Red Army, and these had been so brutal that they'd jeopardized the very defense of the nation during the Great Patriotic War against Hitler (as World War II was known in the USSR). I was afraid David might become yet another victim or, worse yet, act in collusion with the barbarians who were enforcing the so-called dictatorship of the proletariat. I've never been a sympathizer of any kind of dictatorship, and I couldn't believe that this one – even though my brother supported it – could be any less evil than the others.

Stalin's death in 1953 fueled new hopes, but it soon became obvious that any changes would only be minor. The Cold War was a very icy one indeed, and the tension between Western European nations, Japan, and the U.S., on the one hand, and the Eastern European nations of the Soviet bloc was escalating. China had also turned communist, and the possibility of another world conflagration was an ever-greater threat to all.

Still, there were some positive developments in the midst of this complete disarray. The first was the foundation of the United Nations. Then, on May 4, 1948, in the Jewish year of 5708, the U.N. dramatically passed Resolution 181, which proclaimed the independence of the State of Israel. Neither the creation of the State of Israel nor the decision to create an Arab state in Palestine was easy. With the help of the United States and the Soviet Union – in a rare demonstration of agreement – the resistance of the Arab states was overcome, and a tense vote at the fledgling U.N. resulted in 33 for, 10 abstentions, and 13 against Israel's statehood. The two superpowers had been followed by their allies, yielding a reasonable majority.

Brazil's participation was very important, since Osvaldo Aranha was then president of the General Assembly as representative of Brazil. Coincidence or not, this was how Israel and Brazil forged their first ties of respect and friendship.

The day after the declaration of independence, Israel was invaded by the armies of the neighboring countries of Jordan, Egypt, and Syria. It was David against Goliath, and once again the unlikely happened. David won the war, which was truly a matter of life or death. As Jews of the *Diaspora*, far from these battlefields, we were frightened and disoriented. We stayed glued to our short-wave radios, fearing the worst and praying for a miraculous victory. Our choices were to win, or to win. Much to Israel's good fortune, the soldiers from the other side were unmotivated and poorly organized. Moreover, their leaders were weak and usually horribly corrupt. In contrast, we had remarkable leaders like David Ben-Gurion and Golda Meir – and we were fighting for our lives. And so the State of Israel won its right to exist twice: once during the voting at the U.N. and a second time by spilling blood on the battlefield. On May 11, 1949, Israel was finally accepted into the U.N. as a member nation.

The Soviet Union's initial support for Israel didn't last long, and Arab countries soon began receiving Soviet aid and arms. In a way, the new polarization, with the United States supporting Israel and the Soviet Union supporting Arab countries, continues today.

I was worried about the change and how it might affect David, since he had always sympathized with the Zionist movement even though he was a communist. The implications of this paradox were unpredictable. There was no way to discuss the matter in the letters we exchanged, because I knew our correspondences were always opened and read. By then, there was probably a thick dossier ready to be used against me. In the eyes of the paranoid security organs, the mere fact that I lived in a non-communist country constituted a crime.

Things only got worse in subsequent years. David never wrote anything that might compromise him, but I could detect his growing disillusionment between the lines. It was becoming increasingly clear that his enthusiasm over communism's bright future was dwindling.

* * * * *

In the 1950s, Manaus was a quiet and somewhat sleepy town. Business at Berimex was going well. Given the city's tropical pace, there was always time to enjoy endless good conversation with our new friends. While aboard the *Jamaïque*, I'd discovered I had an above-average talent for chess. With a bit more time on my hands, I began studying this marvelous game and spent my Saturdays playing at the Luso Sporting Clube. There I met a young intellectual who would one day be the world's greatest expert on the Amazon: Samuel Benchimol, historian, sociologist, professor, writer, and successful businessman. He authored several books, which still stand as a complete guide to the region's social, cultural, and economic formation.

I had actually been introduced to Samuel some time before we met at the chess club. At the floating dock next to the Manaus Harbor roadway, I serviced Panair do Brasil's and Pan America's hydroplanes, which carried passengers as well as the rubber that was so important to the U.S. During those same wee hours of the morning, Samuel was a baggage checker on that dock. At the end of this shift, he'd go to law school. After that, he'd do a shift at a small company he and his brothers had set up. And then at night, he taught political economy at the Solon de Lucena School of Commerce. When I got to know him better, I learned that what he really liked was teaching, researching, and writing; the rest he did out of pure necessity. Back then, he was finishing up his first book, *O cearense na Amazônia*, which looks at the settlement of the empty Amazon by migrants from the state of Ceará, in northeastern Brazil. Years later, Berta and I gained a better understanding of what had taken place in the Amazon after rubber appeared by reading Benchimol's works, especially *Amazônia: Um pouco-antes e além-depois*, an exploration of the history of the region and what the future might bring, and *Eretz Amazônia: Os judeus na Amazônia*, which was about Jewish immigration.

The various ethnic groups that had settled the region over the course of the previous 100 years had played a variety of social and economic roles. In the early days of the rubber industry, the bulk of the companies in Belém and Manaus were owned by Portuguese immigrants. Drawn by the dream of hitting it rich, they were pioneers in organizing the exchange system known as *"aviador" houses*, companies that sold on credit to the interior of the Amazon. Both state capitals became commercial warehouses where the Portuguese established lines of operation for supplying merchandise to rubber barons and rubber tappers alike. The merchants were paid in *"pélas"* – as balls of rubber were called – in addition to Brazil nuts and other goods produced by the region's extractive plant industries, most of which were exported. These same Portuguese merchants formed the predominant political class and were major business leaders too.

Meanwhile, the northeasterners who had been forced out by drought and were seeking their own prosperous life in the Amazon headed deep into the interior and settled there. It was a long and rocky road for them and one that only led to economic, social, and political ascent in scant cases. They all started out as displaced refugees and heavily indebted rubber tappers. Over time, thanks to their dynamic spirit and drive, the most prosperous among them did become wealthy landowners, traveling merchants, or rubber barons, but the vast majority were not as lucky and continued to live in poverty.

The Amazon welcomed these people, and they, in turn, enriched the culture of the Amazon and made it even more Brazilian. Both the rubber barons and the Portuguese owners of the aviador houses earned big money producing and marketing rubber, but they had another source of income too: the sale of goods and services at exorbitant prices to the rubber tappers, who sank so far into debt that they were veritable indentured servants. Rubber tappers commenced their lives in the Amazon paying off debts and quite often would die owing even more. From the time they left the northeast, where they borrowed money to buy their tickets, a rifle, bullets, and a few supplies, to when they met their sad end as victims of violence – felled by the arrows of Native Americans, snakebites, ambushes, crimes of blood and passion, or tropical disease, usually malaria or yellow fever – most of the migrants only descended further into debt. It's no overstatement to say that the rubber tapper was a man who spent his life paying a high price to have the right to work himself into slavery.

Seeking their own place in the production chain, Jewish and Syrian-Lebanese immigrants courageously defied the economic might and ruthless system of the aviador houses, which had ties to the rubber barons. Journeying by river, the new immigrants transported merchandise in rickety vessels and dared to sell them to the tappers in exchange for rubber, animal hides and fur, Brazil nuts, copaiba balsam, and other regional goods. Because the traveling Jewish and Arab merchants sold directly at lower prices while buying at higher prices, they were decisive in breaking the monopoly of the aviador houses and the rubber barons. So it was no surprise that they were hated and were often the victims of violence, in addition to being accused of unfair competition.

* * * * *

One evening in March 1953, I arrived home later than usual and saw that Berta was anxious to talk to me. Daniel was asleep, and she was rocking Sara, who was already 5. A news addict, I went over to the radio and turned it on. Sara was soon fast asleep, and Berta joined me.

"Guess who was at Berimex today looking for enough parts for a battalion."

I said I had no idea, and she went on.

"That German fellow who's the manager of something or other at I.B.Sabbá. He bought some parts and ordered some others that we didn't have in stock. I think he was satisfied, in part because he could speak German to me."

"That's wonderful, Berta! They're the biggest company in Manaus, and I'd love to have them as a client."

I'd been observing the notable growth of I.B.Sabbá with a keen eye for some time. After the British, French, and German companies had left and the biggest of the aviador houses had gone into decline – like J.G.Araujo and B. Levy & Cia – I.B.Sabbá had put a new business model in place. They stood out from their competitors, because they offered the same products but with a much greater aggregate value: shelled Brazil nuts, dried fruit from the cow tree, planed lumber, washed and processed rubber, filtered copaiba, and top-quality rosewood essential oil, all nicely packaged and sold at an attractive price. The company's facilities for Brazil nut production, their exemplary rubber processing plant, and the other businesses run by the group had made them into the largest employer in Manaus, and other businesses were trying to copy their model.

"There's something else you're going to find interesting," Berta pressed on. "They want someone who can help open up the export market for regional products, which is their forte. And you fit the profile of this someone. They want a person who speaks and writes English, German, and Spanish well and has both business acumen and a sense of ethics."

I pondered this a moment and then replied, "Berta, this would be a once-in-a-lifetime opportunity to learn the business, one that seems very promising, even with the demise of the rubber boom. It's a shame I can't accept. I can't renege on my commitment to Panair. Besides, we've got Berimex to look after."

"I know all that, but I still think we should hear them out. Your deal with Panair is almost over, not to mention that Ponta Pelada Airport is fully functional now and Varig and Cruzeiro airlines want to fly into Manaus. Can I set up a meeting for tomorrow afternoon?" she insisted, ever the pragmatist.

"I don't want to do anything wrong. It wouldn't be ethical to take the position, learn the secrets of the trade, and then open up a business as a competitor, taking advantage of my knowledge of their products, suppliers, and clients."

"Licco Hazan, you'd think you didn't know me! I'm not suggesting anything unethical, just a frank conversation. We're not going to hide anything. And to tell the truth, I've already scheduled tomorrow's meeting."

I was keenly aware of one thing: when Berta wanted something, you had better get out of the way!

And so we met Isaac Sabbá, a remarkable figure in the history of Manaus, an entrepreneur with a messianic vision, and a commendable human being. Our meeting was with him and his young nephew, Moyses Israel, then the firm's CEO. We told them our story, and they soon made us an offer that undoubtedly represented a formidable challenge.

Berta cut straight to the question that was bothering us. "My husband is hesitant about accepting your offer, because we've actually been contemplating exporting regional products ourselves for a while now. We're not going to hide the fact that one day we'd like to have our own business, and that means I.B.Sabbá might be concerned about a conflict of interest. We don't want to do anything illicit or unethical. We're new here in town, and we need to protect our good name."

"I've also got time constraints, because I'm rendering services to Panair, and I can't break my contract now," I added.

"Let's see if we can reach an agreement that will be to your liking," Moyses said. "Your hours here at I.B.Sabbá can be flexible. From what I understand, you work a lot at night. You could work shorter hours for us – say, from 8 o'clock to 3 in the afternoon. When you have a problem to take care of at the airport, you could make up the hours here some other day."

Two things were clear from our conversation. First, they really needed someone like me, who could get sales rolling abroad where other languages were necessary. Second, I'd evidently made a good impression. Isaac Sabbá hadn't opened his mouth, but I felt like I'd passed the test.

Then, in an affable tone, Sabbá spoke up, concluding our conversation: "Mr. Hazan, I propose that you work with us for at least four years. After that time is up, I'd have no objection if you opened your own business and, within the bounds of good ethics, used what you'd learned with us. We're building a refinery with our earnings on the export of regional products. There's a lot of work to be done, and you can be quite helpful. You too, Mrs. Hazan. We need conscientious, honest, capable people."

The meeting brought an unexpected bonus: Berta was hired to work four hours a day at the company's accounting office. I'd be an assistant to the directors. It was all like a bolt out of the blue.

It wasn't easy to organize our schedules to fit the new status quo. To our good fortune, Gustavo was not just a good tradesman; he was also a sharp businessman. In 1954, we gave him 10 percent equity in Berimex, making him our partner. By then, we had eight employees, besides Gustavo and Berta. I was only called in when there was some mechanical trouble that Gustavo couldn't handle himself, and that hardly ever happened. Berta had been spending a few hours a day at Berimex, but now she was needed more at home to raise and educate Daniel and Sara. None of this would have been possible without Gustavo, particularly our work at I.B.Sabbá.

Everything I know about regional products – Brazil nuts, copaiba, tonka beans, rosewood, jute, mallow, and timber – I owe to my internship at that firm. It was like getting a college degree. We threw our hearts into our work, often going well beyond the close of the business day, caught up by Isaac Sabbá's enthusiasm, our own desire to do a good job, and the idea of paying for a refinery under construction. It was an epic struggle, the product of the obstinacy, will power, motivation, and courage of that fine entrepreneur. Whenever he comes to my mind, I recall a quotation from Albert Einstein: "There is a driving force more powerful than steam, electricity, and atomic energy: the will."

Given how much was being invested, there were only two possible outcomes for this story: either the group would become even more successful, or it would simply go bankrupt. We accomplished a lot in 1955 and 1956, with the whole team working as hard as it could, as if the business belonged to each and every one of us. The refinery came onstream in September 1956 and was inaugurated by Brazilian President Juscelino Kubitschek on January 3, 1957. As a result, the price of fuel dropped sharply: gas prices fell 21 percent and oil diesel, a startling 58 percent. Freight costs plummeted as well. And the Amazon interior was economically viable once again.

Isaac Sabbá thus built the first refinery in Manaus during the 1950s by investing earnings made on the sale of regional products from the Amazon interior. Now, more than 60 years later, if someone wanted to start a new business using the paltry profits earned on all economic activities in the Amazon interior (excluding the Urucu onshore oil reserves), the best he or she could accomplish would be something extremely modest, perhaps half a dozen gas stations. Today, the vast Amazon interior is in a state of decay, and people there have no prospects for the future. Instead, they find themselves living more and more in the middle of a sterile ecological reserve, where there's no room for humans.

In the mid-20th century, the interior of the state of Amazonas held almost four times as many people as Manaus. Today, the situation is reversed. Despite the state's enormous size – nearly 600,000 square miles in area – the capital has more inhabitants than the interior. This imbalance is worsening, and the state and federal governments are not doing enough. Somewhere along the road, we took a wrong turn, and we stubbornly refuse to turn back.

During the course of all these changes, in April 1955, the sad news came that the most enlightened man of our century had died, my longstanding idol Albert Einstein. Berta and I always clipped out stories about the great man and quotations attributed to him, a habit I've never lost. Around the same time, we received news that made us very happy: we were granted Brazilian citizenship. Until that point, Brazilian bureaucracy had always been a stone in our shoe, and on more than one occasion, we'd had to resort to bribery to get something simple done. The legal process for registering Berimex had been a form of bureaucratic torture. I'd had to recall the advice of my friend Salvator yet again: "Whenever someone stronger than you abuses you physically or mentally, don't react. Remember it's a nightmare that will be over, and what matters is surviving. Everything will be even easier yet if you imagine your jailer seated on a toilet, his pants around his ankles, writhing in pain from a violent bout of diarrhea." In this case, my 'jailer' had been a corrupt internal revenue agent, and I'd imagined him crawling his way to the distant bathroom. Salvator was right; it brought instant relief.

If it hadn't been for the help of our friends and the famous Brazilian *"jeitinho"* – devising an ingenious way around a problem – I think Berimex would still be entangled in red tape today. Our newly acquired citizenship was an immense help in ensuring our rights, because it made us Brazilians both *de facto* and *de jure* and therefore less vulnerable to the abuse of power by bureaucrats. We had overcome yet another major hurdle in the life of immigrants.

There was another piece of good news that left all Brazilians euphoric in 1958. In far-off Sweden, Brazil won the World Cup for the first time and also captivated the planet with its irreverent, carefree style of soccer. It was a huge achievement for a poor Third World nation, which found itself thrust onto the international stage. Excitement reigned, as the celebrations even outdid those at the close of World War II. Better yet, this historical feat was repeated four years later in Chile, where without the injured Pelé, Garrincha led the way. We were the best in the world! Brazil was no longer merely the land of coffee and Carnival but now the land of soccer, the globe's most popular sport.

Two years after we'd won the Cup in Stockholm, Brasilia was inaugurated in April 1960, earning Brazil fame as the country with the new and modern federal capital. The world was fascinated by the city and its revolutionary architecture. Bit by bit, the cornerstones were being laid for the development of South America's sleeping giant.

I worked at I.B.Sabbá for nearly five years until 1957, when the group was at the height of its success and the refinery was revolutionizing the local economy. My commitment to Panair ended at the same time, since the company began using the Lockheed Constellation and other more modern aircraft at Ponta Pelada. Planes were evolving fast, and it was evident that servicing them would demand total and exclusive commitment, including a lengthy period of training in São Paulo, far from home and not in my plans. Airlines already had their own maintenance crews at big centers, and it wouldn't be long before this would be the case in Manaus too. My days as a mechanic were over.

CHAPTER X

The essential Amazon

Berta left I.B.Sabbá a few months before I did. It was the year of Daniel's bar mitzvah, and she felt she needed to devote more time to him and Sara. In addition, we hadn't given up on our dream of starting our own export business.

By that point, I'd gotten to know a large part of the interior of the Amazon. I'd traveled upriver by boat to Iquitos, Peru, and then taken the Solimões River downstream to Manaus, following the same trail that Francisco de Orellana had journeyed more than 400 years earlier. He was the first man to travel the mighty river's entire watercourse, from the Andes to the Atlantic Ocean. No matter how hard I strained my imagination, I couldn't spy a single woman who resembled the *icamiabas* – the indigenous hunter women who, according to the account by Orellana's traveling companion Gaspar de Carvajal, had dominated much of the region. King Carlos V of Spain, after reading the explorers' reports, had been reminded of the Amazon women of Greek mythology and had linked their name forever to the great river. Even though the newcomers found no trace of the warrior women of Ancient Greece, the wild, far-off lands of the Amazon evoked a glorious indigenous past. A glance at the ground along the riverbanks revealed pieces of ceramic and other vestiges of a civilization much older than ours, one that no longer existed.

On another occasion, I went down the Amazon to Santarém, this time with Berta – as I had promised her on our first trip from Belém to Manaus. We spent a few restful days with Daniel and Sara on the beach of fine, white sand at Alter do Chão, where we reveled in the transparent, green waters of the Tapajós.

As charming as I find Santarém, my favorite spot in the interior of the state of Amazonas has always been Maués. It was always wonderful to work in that quiet little place, which had its own marvelous white sand beaches. There was an abundance of rosewood and copaiba trees near the heart of downtown, not to mention the best guarana in the world. A good friend of mine, Zanoni Magaldi, still lives there, and he knows more about rosewood essence than anyone else. He was my first and primary supplier of regional products, and although he is much younger than me, we have always had a great relationship.

Not long ago, I promised Zanoni, and myself, that I'd visit the town one last time. It would be worth the effort of getting there just to admire the world's largest plantation of rosewood trees, owned by the Magaldi family, and also the much smaller neighboring plantation that still belongs to us. We have a small farm on the property that continues to be fully operational. The caretaker keeps the house tidy and plants a few trees every year. The one thing that has changed is that I simply haven't been there in a good long while.

The two plantations that I helped establish in 1989 constitute my most valuable legacy. I'm proud to have been one of the first to think in terms of sustainability, following in the tradition of Professor Samuel Benchimol. That was more than 20 years ago, before it had become fashionable.

All this aside, my memories of this wonderful place are a bit unsettling for me. I know that when I go back, I'll listen in vain for the familiar voices and happy laughter from the days when I was young and could enjoy life more. Still, it will be worth fulfilling my promise, no matter how painful it might be. The right time for my visit will be when I finish this story.

On August 22, 1957, Berta and I opened Amazon Flower Fragrâncias Ltda., our export firm. We didn't have much capital, and we started out with only two products: copaiba balsam and rosewood essential oil. We later expanded to include tonka beans; found in the Óbidos area, they're prized for their intense aroma. Our new business, as its name suggests, focused on aroma-related products in general and not just those used by the perfume industry. The idea dated from our time in Belém, when we had been fascinated by the number of fragrances sold at Ver-o-Peso Market.

We used our savings to buy an old house on Miranda Leão Street, near the port. It was our first piece of property, so naturally I remember how proud we were. There we began our modest export business as a tiny little firm. Zanoni hunted down the products requested by our clients and also produced essential oil from rosewood trees at his small distillery. And so we commenced our life as exporters on Miranda Leão, packaging our products, shipping them, and receiving payments from the four corners of the world.

A good share of our potential buyers were located in New York and Grasse, the French city of perfumes. We soon realized that if we were to win our clients' trust, we had to meet them personally and understand the needs of each one, so we could offer even better service than our well-established competitors. We scheduled a long trip, first from Manaus to Rio de Janeiro, then on to Paris and Sofia, and, last, to New York, all for after Daniel's bar mitzvah.

The ceremony was a tremendous moment in our lives,

for it's not every day that your son celebrates his bar mitzvah! The event requires great preparation and studying on the part of the boy, who reads long excerpts from the Torah in Ancient Hebrew in front of the congregation for the first time. In the life of a young Jewish man, it's a vitally important rite of passage, one that contributes decisively to the development of his self-confidence and his personality. Moreover, it's the only party that Jewish parents ever give for their sons; in the case of daughters, this moment is their wedding.

The occasion also demands a great deal from the parents. We wanted to pay tribute to all our new friends in the Manaus community – Jewish, Christian, and Muslim – and that meant our guest list was quite long. There was a party following the religious ceremony at synagogue, a simple affair but for a large number of people, lovingly planned by Berta. We had guests from Maués and Parintins, and Moyses and Débora Bentes even came from Belém. It was an important day for our small family.

After the celebration in honor of Daniel's coming of age, we hit the road. The trip wasn't merely a chance to cement our ties with our main clients; it was also a fantastic opportunity to meet with Nissim and David in Europe and to see the Farhi family again, this time in New York. We got real enjoyment out of planning it. It was fun scheduling get-togethers, making plane and hotel reservations, letting everyone know we were coming, and, above all, dreaming. We would stop in Rio de Janeiro on our way, the city of my friend Salvator's dreams. It was a wish come true.

"Licco, before we go, let's buy ourselves some white clothes so we can parade down Copacabana Beach decked out in white, like Salvator wanted to," Berta suggested.

"Of course! And I'm even going to indulge in the purchase of a Panama hat. That will make our walk along Copacabana complete."

I still have some photographs of our first visit to the "marvelous city," as Brazilians call it. Berta and I, then a young couple, are standing in front of the Copacabana Palace hotel, dressed elegantly in white. I've kept my Panama hat, now misshapen and yellowed by time, as a memento of those happy days.

We met Nissim in Paris. He was living in Madrid and had earned his Spanish citizenship. He had married a tall, comely Spanish woman named Maria Luiza, and they had a young boy. Nissim told us he'd sold his pharmaceutical business for a good price, leaving him with plenty of time and money.

I was sad to discover that he was trying to blot out his Jewish past, just like many others after World War II. Nissim was now going by the name of Nicolas. After experiencing so much trauma, cruelty, and unjust suffering, many people refused to believe in God; they felt the Lord had completely abandoned them when they needed the Lord most. It's no wonder that there are still so few of us in the world despite our 5,000-year history. After the war, many people thought life would be easier if they sank into anonymity and hid their true roots. In practice, however, that's not how it went: they were no longer Jewish when it came to good things, but they remained Jewish when it came to the bad. Whenever anti-Semites go on a witch hunt for Jews, they'll search back five generations or more, like Hitler. In my life, I've learned that no matter how much you want to distance yourself from your roots, the ethical, moral, and religious values acquired during your youth become such a strong part of you that you'll never be happy if you turn your back on them. You can take the caboclo out of the fields, but you can't take the fields out of the caboclo.

Our first four days in France were packed with work, but we also had a chance to see a bit of Paris. We had luck with the weather. It was an incomparable pleasure to sit at a bistro on the Champs Elysées and watch as a diverse parade of people walked by. I can say the same about spending the night at the Lido or Moulin Rouge, watching shows and breathing the same air as Toulouse-Lautrec and Cézanne.

We fell in love with the city, but our priority was still Bulgaria. I invited Nissim to go to Sofia with us, and he agreed on the spot. We were greatly relieved he'd accepted, since, I must confess, we were feeling anxious and quite insecure, not knowing what to expect from my brother, from our other friends, or from communist Bulgaria 20 years after our escape. With Nissim and Maria Luiza along, it would be easier to face our homeland.

We had no trouble obtaining our visas to Bulgaria at the consulate in Paris. We caught a Russian-made plane on Balkan Airlines for a two-and-a-half-hour flight to Sofia. Coming in over the city, I gazed out the plane window at the landscape below, so familiar and yet so different. A strange sensation gripped me. In my memory, Sofia sat at the foot of Vitosha, a huge mountain that now appeared to have shrunk considerably.

We were nervous as we went through customs, but things went smoothly. We picked up our luggage and entered Bulgaria. Only David was there waiting for us. My God! He looked more and more like our father – a little balder perhaps, but in good physical shape. He was no longer the boy I'd practically raised. I hadn't seen him since our goodbye in the middle of a snowstorm in Somovit. As I recalled that day, I found it impossible to hold back my tears. I took out a handkerchief and dried my face and David's, just as I'd done when we were children. After all, I'd been his older brother and his father too. Despite the distances between us in terms of time and space, our bond remained incredibly strong.

When we got to our hotel, I asked about Irina and Oleg. David explained that they were in Moscow with her parents. It was a shame we wouldn't be able to meet them. It soon became obvious that my brother was well known and a person of prestige. At the exclusive Balkan Hotel, the staff greeted him with a certain reverence; it was clear he was a frequent visitor there.

Across from the hotel stood Sveta Nedelya Cathedral, the same church where they had tried to murder Tsar Boris 40 years before. A little ways beyond that, you could see the minaret of the mosque and the dome of the great synagogue. As if reading my mind, David hurried to say, "The synagogue has been closed for some time."

"I don't like the architecture of the new buildings downtown," Nissim remarked, referring to our hotel, as well as to the ZUM department store and the Communist Party headquarters, both on the main square. True to the Stalinist style, the structures were graceless and unsightly, and they didn't blend in with anything around them. We later visited the mausoleum of Georgi Dimitrov, the first communist leader after the end of the war, across from the tsar's old palace.

"My political ideal is democracy. 'Let every man be respected as an individual and no man idolized,'" Berta said adamantly, quoting Einstein.

I was surprised that her remark didn't seem to irritate David. He already liked Berta a lot and was more patient with her than with me or Nissim. But although he said nothing right then, over dinner, he voiced this polite comeback: "Forgive me, but listening to your comments, you'd think you live in some kind of democratic paradise. Generalissimo Franco is not exactly one of the good guys, voted in through direct elections, and Brazil doesn't have such a shining history either."

David was undoubtedly right, but Bulgarian reality soon revealed itself to be even worse. Dimitrov's mausoleum was only one of the symptoms.

Nissim surprised us all by tracking down one of our friends from the German school. This sparked the idea of organizing a dinner at our hotel and inviting all the friends we could locate. On the day of the scheduled event, hotel security barred our friends at the door to the restaurant. Indignant, we asked for an explanation and were politely told that the hotel restaurant was solely for foreign guests. David arrived in the middle of our heated discussion with the restaurant manager. Nissim was so upset that he just kept sputtering away. In an effort to orchestrate a truce, David begged our patience and stepped away to talk to the manager alone for a few minutes. We saw them telephone someone, and then, at long last, our friends were allowed to enter the restaurant.

The night had gotten off to a bad start, and it went downhill from there. After an exchange of hugs, we had a few drinks. Then, the conversation heated up. Plamen Varbanos, a childhood friend of mine, began complaining in a loud voice. "It's a crime! Your average citizen doesn't have any rights in this so-called 'People's' Republic of Bulgaria. As if poverty weren't enough! Even if we can afford it, we aren't free to patronize the restaurants and hotels in our own country. Now we've got castes in Bulgaria! The communist caste and the caste of the pariahs. Without making any bones about it, the communists simply introduced a despicable system of privileges for themselves, justice be damned."

I could tell David was getting quite nervous, so I broke in on Plamen's rant. Berta and Nissim also sensed the predicament we were getting ourselves in, and together we shifted the topic away from the state of affairs in communist Bulgaria. Nonetheless, some of our friends were fearful of later retaliation, so they excused themselves early. It was good to see them again, but we were left with a strange, bitter taste in our mouths.

The next day, the restaurant manager tried to apologize. "Mr. Hazan," he said, "I hope you understand that I was just following orders last night. It's a good thing you didn't let that friend of yours go on talking like that, because my staff and I are obliged to report any unpatriotic attitudes to the authorities.

To tell the truth, we shouldn't have let your group dine in the restaurant. Luckily, we didn't overhear any subversive talk."

We spent another two days in Bulgaria, without pursuing any further thorny discussions about life there. Instead, we became discreet, everyday tourists. We visited the building of the American Car Company, now occupied by a municipal agency. We went up Vitosha to Aleko Station, and the day after that, we went to Rila Monastery, a holy site for all Bulgarians.

The time came for Berta and me to continue our trip. Only David accompanied us to the airport, just as he'd done on our arrival. As we exchanged a final hug, I realized my brother was unhappy.

"David, you can always count on us, whatever you may need," Berta said in farewell. My wife was sensitive, and I knew she'd also noticed that something was wrong with my brother.

David surprised us with his ensuing confession. "I didn't have the courage to say anything before, but Irina and I have separated. She took Oleg to Moscow. I haven't gotten used to the loneliness. I miss them so much. I don't know what's going to happen now."

My brother suddenly seemed very frail and weary. This made him look even more like our father, and that touched me deeply.

"David, my dear brother" I managed to say, "We're your family. There's still time for you to rebuild your life, and we're going to do everything we can to make you happy. Why don't you come live with us in Brazil?"

"Impossible," he replied. "My life is here, and there's Oleg too..."

Once on board the plane, Berta grabbed my hand and whispered in my ear, "Licco darling, it's no use feeling sad.

We'll have lots of other chances to help David."

In New York, we went to visit the Farhi family right away, before seeing our clients. The Farhis lived in a big apartment across the street from Central Park, a prime Manhattan location. On the morning that we were received for breakfast with the whole family, we were still a bit jetlagged from our long trip. There was Leon Farhi, a lot older than I'd remembered him; his wife, Ester, as healthy as ever; his children, (comma) Saul and Eva; and two people we'd never met. The last two turned out to be Saul's wife and Eva's husband. Since they didn't speak any Bulgarian, they left after breakfast so the rest of us would feel more at ease to talk.

Farhi was clearly anxious for news of Bulgaria, and I wasted no time telling him about the latest events. Ester, Saul, and Eva knew Berta from way back and wanted to hear about the few family friends who had stayed in Bulgaria. Most Bulgarian Jews had managed to immigrate to Israel in 1948, and many had moved to Haifa. They owned restaurants, newspapers, and even a soccer team there. Very few families had remained in Bulgaria, and it wasn't easy to locate them, since the usual gathering place, the synagogue, had been closed.

"My dear Licco, as you can see, we're New Yorkers now. Saul's wife and Eva's husband are Americans, and our grandkids don't even speak Bulgarian. Wandering from country to country, one generation here, the next one there – that's been the fate of the Jewish people. We feel at home here in New York, surrounded by other Jews, and I hope to stay here a good long while.

Although Farhi was still mentally sharp, the years weighed heavily on him; he had trouble walking and speaking. Not much was left of the energetic, powerful, and charming man I'd known in Sofia. Bulgaria remained important to him, but for the rest of his family, it was a country that had fallen behind the times and was an ever more distant memory.

We spent the day together and had the chance to meet their grandchildren. Ester fixed us a fine Bulgarian lunch that could have competed with the best restaurants in Sofia. And we reminisced about the old days. We thanked them once more for their help and for the decisive support we'd received from their extraordinary family years earlier. It finally came time to say our goodbyes. Farhi was visibly moved, and he hugged me as hard as he could. "My friend, we might never meet again. Not long ago, I had a malignant prostrate tumor operated on."

Saul joined us right then, breaking in. Dad's strong, and he's recovering just fine. Next time we'll meet in Rio for Carnival."

His words weren't convincing. To the contrary, all doubts had been erased. Leon's problem was serious.

We spent a few more days taking in the New York sites, marveling at the busy avenues and the skyscrapers. We worked hard too. Before our departure, we called Saul. Over the phone, he confirmed our suspicions. Despite his father's surgery, our friend hadn't beaten the disease and didn't have much time left. After that phone call, Farhi lived precisely eight months.

* * * * *

We were happy to get back to the home we missed so much. Our trip had lasted just a bit more than a month, but Daniel and Sara were nevertheless a little bigger and more grown-up. Daniel was attending Pedro II State High School, which had a strong reputation. It was close to our house, as was Sara's school, the Amazonas Educational Institute, likewise recognized for its teaching standards. Contrary to the situation in Brazil today, back then, the best schools were the public ones. Even though Manaus lies far from the country's urban hubs, the quality of basic education was very good there. When it came to college, though, it was a whole different story. Given the paucity of choices in the region, young people looked elsewhere for alternatives, outside the Amazon. Their first preferences were the universities in Rio de Janeiro, Recife, and São Paulo.

Progress was slow but steady in Manaus. In early 1962, we opened the doors of the city's new synagogue, Beth Jacob/ Rebi Meyr, which brought together the two strains of Judaism that had divided our small community.

In the early 1960s, Brazil, as a whole, was going through rough times. President Jânio Quadros resigned, blaming hidden forces for the failures of his administration. His vice president, João Goulart, was leading the country in the unmistakable style of a left-wing populist. The student movement and trade unions stepped onto the political stage, much to the worry of more conservative sectors. Moreover, the economic situation was horrendous, featuring shortages, a rising cost of living, and corruption on all sides.

This climate of political crisis and social strife culminated in the 1964 coup d'état. Brazil became a dictatorship with all the attendant ramifications and losses of freedom. The defenders of the new regime – and there were many in the beginning – dubbed the seizure of power a "revolution," but in actual fact, it was an outright military takeover.

"I've been thinking a lot about David," Berta said a few days after the coup. "It seems to me that he had a hunch about these latest events."

"Now, we're even," I replied. "He lives in one dictatorship, and we live in another."

"Still, his is worse," Berta insisted. "We know that nobody in a communist country is allowed to go into exile in another nation. No way! At least our new rulers let a number of people go into exile in France, Chile, and other countries. It wasn't for humanitarian reasons -- just to get rid of them, that's true. And then they concocted that stupid slogan: 'Brazil, love it or leave it.' There's no mollycoddling like that in Bulgaria. Over there, you tell a joke to the wrong audience, and you could get years in prison."

I have to confess that in those days I thought about emigrating yet again. We talked it over at home, but Berta and the children – who were really young adults – opposed the idea, and I was actually delighted with the decision to stay.

As always in our life, even when things weren't going well, some good news would come along. In 1963, Daniel was accepted into the University of São Paulo, where he would major in economics. As a sophomore, he was awarded a Fulbright to continue his studies in the U.S. He'd passed his tests with honors, but he didn't know for sure if that was what he wanted to do.

Around the same time, friends of ours in São Paulo warned me that Daniel was getting involved with leftist militants and running great risks – the military didn't fool around. I was so worried that I hopped the first plane to São Paulo. Thank God, Daniel didn't fight my arguments all that hard, and we were soon on our way to Princeton, where he spent the following years studying. Berta and I breathed a sigh of relief, knowing that our son was safe and sound.

One day some months later, Berta grew pensive. "As parents, we love our children so much that sometimes we don't treat them fairly, just to try to protect them."

"What do you mean?" Her comment bewildered me.

"'The world is a dangerous place to live, not because of the people who are evil, but because of the people who don't do anything about it' – to quote our beloved Einstein. Think about his words. I'm not sure it was such a good idea for us to get Daniel out of Brazil when we did. He was completely right to be disgusted by the dictatorship."

"Berta darling, you're exaggerating. Einstein's wisdom doesn't apply here. I'd do it all over again if need be. Another genius, my friend Salvator, once said: what matters most is surviving!"

"When it comes to our son, I think so too. It's admittedly an egotistical way of thinking, but I agree. Actually, I was just playing a bit of the devil's advocate." She laughed.

Two years later, Sara followed in Daniel's footsteps and was awarded a scholarship to study at the University of California at Berkeley. Our dedication and care – especially Berta's – were yielding good fruit. We could take pride in the fact that our children were attending two top-notch schools: our son was at the university where Einstein had been a professor and our daughter was at the most liberal, progressive school in the U.S.

Attending college in the U.S. is a worthwhile experience not just because of the high quality of university teaching there, but also because of campus life. Spending day after day fraternizing with the brightest young minds from around the world helps to form worthy individuals who are both creative and productive. It's a shame that most Brazilian university campuses have never offered much to their students, who miss out on the chance to live in a healthy, progressive academic environment with their classmates.

In 1967, the Six-Day War broke out in the Middle East. During that lightning war, Israel demonstrated a military might much greater than that of Egypt, Jordan, and Syria combined and thus achieved a resounding victory, occupying important territories in the Sinai, Golan, and Gaza.

My brother, David, who was then living in Sofia, kept up with the conflict in the official Bulgarian press. Years later, he told me that the media, controlled exclusively by the government, broadcast nothing but news about major victories by Arab countries. Despite victory after victory, these "triumphant" armies surrendered on the sixth day, and the surprised citizens of Bulgaria discovered that things hadn't gone quite the way the media had reported them.

In Brazil, the ruling military focused a great deal of attention on the country's shaky infrastructure, previously neglected. They built hydroelectric power plants, ports, airports, and railways, and also cleared and settled the most remote territories. Sometimes, the results were positive; other times, disastrous. This strategy included the establishment of a free trade zone in Manaus in 1967 under then-President General Castello Branco.

The idea of a free trade zone had been proposed 10 years earlier, but it only gained life following the 1964 coup. In my opinion, it was possible to carry out the idea solely because of the geopolitical vision of the armed forces, who were worried about the gigantic demographic void that covered a huge chunk of the Brazilian map. No doubt another major factor was the ease with which government projects could be approved. Be that as it may, Decree-Law 288 created the free trade zone and granted hefty fiscal incentives that would last 30 years. Since then, the FTZ has been the chief driving force behind the local economy. Generally speaking, businesses that set up office there enjoyed federal tax advantages and exemptions in regard to importation, industrialization, and income, in addition to state-level advantages, like a lower value-added tax. The philosophy was to encourage free initiative and eliminate perpetual bureaucratic red tape. Suframa, the agency established to run the free trade zone, was intended to be an efficient, uncomplicated instrument for fostering the region's economic development.

The response to this move was immediate and amazing. The innovative model attracted businessmen and entrepreneurs from Brazil and abroad, who invested capital, brought know-how, and, most importantly, introduced the optimism, drive, and audacity that are typical of a more modern society. For the citizens of the Amazon, it was wonderful to watch Manaus suddenly emerge from the shadows into a new era of prosperity. Economic problems notwithstanding – a negative balance of trade, rising foreign debt, and the gamut of restrictions enforced by the federal government – the positive impact was mind-boggling. Within a few years, hundreds of factories in Manaus were producing television sets, stereos, electronic games, telephones, computers, motorcycles, and watches, creating an abundance of jobs and other opportunities. Both Brazil as a country and the state of Amazonas and its citizens benefited greatly from the plenty produced by these new businesses.

Today, looking at how much was collected in federal, state, and municipal taxes – figures that have multiplied many times over in the last 45 years – it's easy to see that the FTZ was never any kind of tax haven for corporations. Instead, it was always heaven for the tax collectors.

The industrial sector of the Manaus free trade zone made a name for itself and became an object of study; it is still a vital force for the city of Manaus and the state of Amazonas. With hundreds of shops in operation, its commercial sector imported finished goods and resold them to Manaus residents and occasional visitors, but it has all but disappeared. This almost forgotten part of the FTZ played an important role locally from 1970 to 1990, because its merchants were not only major job creators, but also lived and invested all their earnings in the city.

During that timeframe, Manaus drew hordes of tourists who came to purchase imported goods and then took the opportunity to see something of the Amazon. Some historians don't pay much heed to this phenomenon, but as an active importer for 20 years, I know how the city thrived and benefited from this import boom.

By the dawn of the 1970s, Manaus was quite different from the city that Berta and I had moved to 25 years earlier.

It had a reliable power grid, roads were paved even in poorer outlying neighborhoods, trams had been replaced by cars, a number of tall buildings had appeared, and growth was visible.

The city remained isolated by land, but Ponta Pelada Airport was fully functional. I never liked the idea -- pushed by so many politicians -- to build roads in the Amazon. With few exceptions, our roads are already here: the countless navigable rivers that crisscross the region. It's true that there aren't enough channel markers, dredging is substandard, and the port structure should be upgraded to receive passengers and cargo. But the solution is obvious and not very costly.

Ironically, aside from the works left by the British, the city of Manaus has never had a well-built or well-run port, contenting itself instead with makeshift solutions. Things are worse in the interior, where hardly any town is equipped to handle containers, and not a single one has at least a crane to unload heavier cargo. There's no way to stimulate even the most basic of economic activities. Manaus has enjoyed stunning growth since the implementation of the free trade zone despite these glaring shortcomings, while the Amazon's huge interior remains mired in stagnation.

We used the new opportunities afforded by the FTZ to expand our export business to encompass imports as well. Amazon Flower Fragrâncias Ltda. continued to export rosewood essential oil, copaiba balsam, and tonka beans, but also began importing and distributing finished goods (mostly electronics) on the Manaus market.

In those days, it took a lot of work and a great deal of planning to produce rosewood essential oil. In practice, this is how it went: during the dry season, the caboclos living in the forest areas would walk through the woods, marking the rosewood trees. The next step was to wait for the rivers to rise and then fell the marked trees, saw them into logs, and drag them to the streams, where canoes and boats carried the lumber off to the nearest distillery. There, the timber was chipped and steam distilled. The product was a transparent essential oil with a bouquet beyond compare. Its delightful, unmistakable aroma hung over the distilleries and could be smelled far away. It is this distinct fragrance, which is an excellent fixer, that is prized by the cosmetics and perfume industry. Through the late 1990s, nearly 10,000 trees were extracted from the forest each year, gradually hampering access to native trees.

Copaiba balsam is a different kind of product. The leafy copaiba tree stands nearly 100 feet tall, making it easy to spot. It works rather like a milk cow. The caboclo first drills into the trunk about 20 inches above the ground and collects the liquid. Then, he plugs the hole and leaves, returning six months later to repeat the operation. On average, he extracts more than five quarts of balsam per tree each year. In the Amazon, the product is highly valued for its anti-inflammatory properties, while abroad, it is used more by the cosmetics industry and in the production of special paints.

Tonka beans, the third article exported by our company, are gathered in and around the small town of Óbidos during July. Tonka trees can be found in various areas of the Amazon, but the beans from Óbidos are of finer quality and contain a greater amount of coumarin. They are dried in the sun and then placed in jute bags. The aroma from coumarin is used to supplement other fragrances; there is also a good market for it in the tobacco industry.

Alongside this small range of export products, we started importing electronics and electrical appliances in 1970. These two different types of commerce might seem like an odd combination. Our original idea had been to test out the new business and then open up another company solely for import purposes. That never happened, because a few years down the road, import companies became subject to an annual quota that limited their growth, all on account of Brazil's troubled exchange situation. Each company's quota was based on several criteria, including import history, number of employees, taxes paid, and export volume. The last criterion weighed in our favor, and it wouldn't have made sense to separate our two operations into two companies. This system caused a lot of discord among businesses, who always felt they were on the losing side. Suframa, who defined the quotas, tried to fine-tune the criteria over the years, but they never managed to please everyone.

The fact that Berta and I spoke other languages, particularly English, was of great help when it came to developing new business. We chose to stick with wholesale, because it demanded less time, let us keep Berimex in operation, and simultaneously allowed us to export regional products. In the import area, our competitors were much larger companies, some of nationwide repute, like CCE and Evadin, or Moto Importadora and Bemol, who had solid retail operations.

The city drew merchants from all over the world who wanted to try their luck in this promising new market. Brazilians, Argentineans, Uruguayans, Colombians, Americans, Koreans, Chinese, Jews, Arabs, and Indians invested in shops that sold a broad range of products, from trinkets of questionable origin to the latest generation of electronics. For the city's longtime residents, accustomed to a life of peace and quiet, it felt as if the place were going to explode. Suddenly, the Hotel Amazonas and smaller hotels were always booked to capacity, as were the Varig and Vasp planes that arrived crowded with passengers, their suitcases empty and pockets stuffed with cash. Brazilians were dying to buy imported goods, which cost twice as much in São Paulo and Rio de Janeiro.

Amazon Flower Fragrâncias Ltda. took full advantage of this boom in business, while its exports of Amazon products grew as well, albeit more slowly.

CHAPTER XI

David and Oleg: the escape

A Jew alone is a Jew in danger.
Attributed to Elie Wiesel

In 1969, Neil Armstrong stepped onto the moon. In 1970, the Beatles broke up, (comma) and we Brazilians celebrated our third World Cup win.

On the wings of our recent prosperity, and our empty nest, Berta and I decided to travel to Mexico City to catch the final game. We planned everything well in advance, and although we couldn't be sure which team would make it to the finals, we bought our tickets even before they kicked off the entire tournament.

I was so proud when I told my brother in Bulgaria. David had been crazy about soccer ever since he was a child, even more than me. When he wrote back, he said he'd love to join us, but since he couldn't, he'd be watching the games on TV with his son, Oleg, and they'd be cheering for Brazil to reach the finals and take the Cup. To tell the truth, the Brazilian national team hadn't been performing well that year, but with champs like Pelé, Tostão, and Rivelino, anything could happen.

A few days later, my brother let me know that his boss and longtime friend, Bulgaria's vice minister of industry and commerce, would be in Mexico around the same date as we would, on an official visit. David wanted to know what hotel we'd be staying at, so he could ask his boss to take us a bottle of Slivovitz, a kind of Bulgarian plum brandy that I loved. I had time to reply with the name of the hotel, which was the famous Santa Isabel Sheraton.

In Mexico, we cheered Brazil on in its semifinal match against Uruguay, rooting for our team to make it to the big final game. The other semifinal was between Italy and Germany, who battled it out in an incredible duel, with Italy winning 4-3; some still refer to it as the "match of the 20th century." In the days leading up to the final playoff, Berta and I were part of a jubilant multitude of Brazilian revelers, enjoying one long party. On the day before the finals, early in the morning, I was awoken by a phone call from reception.

"Mr. Hazan, good morning. I'm sorry to be ringing you this early, but I've got a gift for you from your brother, David," the caller said in Bulgarian.

"I'll be right down," I replied. I'll meet you in the lobby.

"I'd rather meet you alone in your room, in half an hour, if that's possible."

There was something in his voice that told me it was important, and so I agreed.

Berta got dressed and went down for breakfast, while I waited in our room. Precisely 30 minutes later, someone knocked on our door. There stood a tall, well-built man about my age, smartly dressed and visibly nervous. He said good morning, stepped quickly into the room, and handed me a small package: the blessed Slivovitz, my favorite drink, which David had sent with so much love.

"I'm pleased to meet you," the gentleman said, and

he went on in a rush. "Pardon me for showing up like this so early, but I'd rather no one else knew about our meeting. By coincidence, our delegation is staying at this very same hotel, and you and I wouldn't have the needed privacy in the lobby. Since we don't have much time, I'll go straight to the subject. My name is Nikolai Chernev, and I'm your brother's immediate boss. I'm here in Mexico to finalize the first part of a trade agreement between Bulgaria and Mexico. Not long from now, sometime before the end of the year, David will come to spend a few months here in Mexico on business, because I'm putting him in charge of the project. We've been friends since the resistance, when we were young idealists. I owe him a great deal, and I think the feeling is mutual."

"I know. David always talks about you."

"I can't share everything with him. Some of what I'm going to tell you has to stay just between us. If anyone should ever ask about our meeting and what we talked about, I'm going to deny ever having met you, Licco. It's a question of life or death for David, but for me as well."

I was getting impatient. "You can count on me. Come on, tell me what this is all about."

"You need to meet David as soon as he gets to Mexico, and you've got to convince him not to return to Bulgaria. I have good reason to believe that he may be arrested at any moment and accused of spying, treason, or something along those lines. After the last war in the Middle East, things got rough for him, particularly because he's never hidden his Zionist sympathies. Don't ask me how I know, but I'm sure about what I'm saying, and that's why I'm going to send David here and give him a chance to save himself. It's the only thing I can do for him. It'll be up to you to convince him to stay, without mentioning my name. It won't be easy, but you can't fail him."

"What's going to happen with his son?" I asked anxiously.

"I don't know. Oleg's living with David now and studying at Sofia University, St. Kliment Ohridski. David might try to bring him along, but I sincerely doubt they'll let him. They might let Oleg visit his father during school vacation. David is in grave danger, and he should be our No. 1 priority right now."

Nikolai stood up. It was clear our conversation was over.

"Good luck tomorrow. We're all cheering for Brazil."

I didn't really know whom "we all" referred to, but I thanked him, still reeling. Nikolai seemed relieved that our meeting was over and left the room with hurried steps. I saw him head down the stairs instead of taking the elevator. "These guys are afraid of their own shadows," I thought. "The Bulgarian delegation must have more folks from the state security forces than actual businessmen."

One of the last times I'd talked with David, he had in fact mentioned his friend Nikolai Chernev, an extremely brave man who feared nothing and no one. But this description was in stark contrast with the sad, frightened, hurried gentleman I'd met that morning.

Berta and I were edgy as we watched the start of the final match, but our feelings soon turned to pride and happiness. For 90 minutes, we set aside all our worries and celebrated with thousands of other Brazilian fans and Mexican fans who were rooting for Brazil. We hadn't just won the Cup for the third time in history; we'd given a patent demonstration of how our spontaneous joy could infect even our opponents' fans. It was great to be Brazilian!

Brazil's victory was a blessing for the ruling military. A wave of exaggerated patriotism swept over the country. Even God was declared to be Brazilian. But the excitement didn't last long before we went back to our harsh reality. Without radical change, good education for everyone, freedom, and democracy, we wouldn't go far. Brazil's authoritarian government had put the country on the path to stability and given it a sounder economic foundation, but it was at the cost of disproportionately heavy foreign indebtedness. The positive phase didn't last long, and we – especially the poorest among us – were soon castigated by unbridled inflation. Speculating became more profitable than working.

* * * * *

Nikolai Chernev was right about almost everything that happened after that, except for one essential detail: the timing. David was arrested at the airport in Sofia when he was boarding for Mexico, much earlier than Nikolai had anticipated. Back in Manaus, we knew nothing about it and were waiting for news so we could schedule our next trip to Mexico. Since we heard nothing, we tried calling Oleg, but the connection was always so bad that we soon gave up. I managed to talk to Nissim, who was still living in Madrid, and some days later, he uncovered the awful truth. It was a huge shock for us, and I couldn't stop blaming myself for not warning my brother in time.

I sank into a deep depression, which was only alleviated when my children, Daniel and Sara, came back from the U.S. Berta denied it, but I know she told them to return in the hopes that it would cure my blues. Daniel had graduated a while before and was working at an international bank in New York. Sara had just finished her studies. The question was whether they would want to remain in Manaus or if they'd rather live in the U.S. now. The choice had to be theirs. And to my delight, they both decided to stay here.

Months later, we received a letter from Oleg. The only thing he said was that his father had been sentenced to four years behind bars for revealing Bulgarian technological secrets to private Western firms. The accusation was so vague, juvenile, and downright outrageous that it was sickening. My nephew also said David was working in prison; (semi-colon) every two days of labor would take one day off his prison time, reducing his total sentence to 32 months. As I read Oleg's letter over, I recalled the conversation David and I had at the labor camp nearly 30 years earlier, when he announced his plans to escape because he couldn't stand the slavery we were forced to endure. I could imagine the frustration he felt, proud and idealistic, accused of treason by the very regime he helped to build. What cruel irony.

David was released in April 1973, so we promptly scheduled a trip to Bulgaria for the whole family in May. I needed to talk to my brother, meet Oleg, and, most importantly, help them define their future. We didn't feel safe communicating by letter, since his mail was probably read and analyzed by the state security organs. Besides, it was a chance to show our children Bulgaria for the first time. May is always a lovely month in that part of Europe. The temperature is pleasant, there's not much rain, and flowers are blooming all around, especially in the Rose Valley.

We were very nervous, because my brother had gone from authority figure to enemy of the state. Our arrival in Sofia was just as emotional as it had been the previous time. And our reunion with David and Oleg was one of those moments that I'll never forget. David was a little thinner and balder, but appeared healthy. It didn't look like he'd suffered too dreadfully in prison. We liked Oleg very much right from the start (period). He was a sweet, polite boy. Despite Oleg's very poor Ladino and my children's inability to speak Bulgarian, the cousins managed to communicate, forging a friendship that continues today. I was a happy man once again.

Our days in Bulgaria were very pleasant. We spent a whole day on Mount Vitosha, just as we used to do 40 years earlier. It afforded us an unbeatable opportunity to talk without fear that some stranger might try to eavesdrop. It was quite likely that we were being followed at the hotel, but there was no way to install microphones on the mountain or for someone to sneak up on us.

"David, my dear brother, we're all so happy to see that you're well," I said. "Now that we can talk, tell me what your plans are from here."

"Licco, it's great to see you again," he replied. I've always been a fan of Berta, and now I'm a fan of your children too. "What's done is done. I'll go back to work soon. I won't be given any important post, maybe something at the Kremikovtzi Steel Mill. Officially, there's no unemployment in Bulgaria, so they'll have to find something for me to do. As an 'enemy of the people,' I can't hope for very much."

I could feel he was starting to choke up. As delicate as the moment was, I tried to think in practical terms. "No favorable wind blows for somebody who doesn't know where he wants to go. We've got to decide your destination as quickly as we can. Would you both be interested in leaving Bulgaria and coming to Brazil?"

"Licco, I don't want to leave one dictatorship behind to live under another one. I've talked things over with Oleg, and we think that if we leave Bulgaria, it would be best to go to Israel. That is, if we get permission to emigrate, which is unlikely right now. There's no future left for me in Bulgaria. I know I'll be 'rehabilitated' some day, but I can't wait that long. My biggest concern is Oleg, who's about to graduate in engineering; he'll need a job. One thing's for sure: he's not going to land anything good here as the son of a traitor."

"Wherever you go," Berta added, "Licco and I are going to help. But aren't you going to miss your mother, Oleg?"

"No doubt about that," Oleg said. "My mother remarried and has two small children. My parents don't get along; they don't talk to each other. It's very hard for me, but I've made peace with it. Dad needs me a lot more than Mom does. I'm going to stay with him."

It was decided that David and Oleg would request passports to visit us in Brazil, a request that was more likely to be honored than asking permission to move to Israel. In the meantime, I was going to study the alternatives, including the possibility that they'd have to flee the country.

Back in Sofia, nobody made any further comment about what had been decided. We took the opportunity to stop by our old apartment, where David and Oleg were living. Almost nothing had changed – the same old furniture, the same paint, the same Gobelins tapestries, now timeworn and in poor repair. The only new things were a refrigerator and an Opera television, a Bulgarian brand.

"We watched the Finals in Mexico on this TV," Oleg said. We couldn't pick you out in the crowd at Azteca stadium, but we were cheering like mad!"

I could tell we'd been part of that young man's life long before we ever met him, even though we hadn't even been aware of it. I promised myself I'd do everything I could to get David and Oleg out of Bulgaria and give them a chance to rebuild their lives. I had to act fast. David was almost 50. I remembered a phrase someone had once quoted from Graham Greene: "When you're old enough to know the way, there's nowhere left to go." Luckily, we still had some time.

There was a little more of Bulgaria to show Daniel and Sara, so we decided to travel to Veliko Tarnovo, the country's capital during the Middle Ages. We went with a tourist guide who turned out to be a regular historian. We spent two days learning about the glorious era of medieval Bulgaria and viewing traces of the ancient civilizations preserved in this corner of the Balkans, some going as far back as 5000 B.C. Our guide had a real talent for conveying complex historical facts in a few words. We heard about how the country came to be, in the year 681, and about the two Bulgarian Empires, each of which ruled all the Balkans. In 1393, however, Bulgaria fell to the Turkish army, and remained part of the Ottoman Empire for 500 long years.

"Incredible!" Sara exclaimed. "What a rich history this country has."

Our guide smiled. "What I'm telling you is merely a summary of a summary of our history. I'm trying to teach a class to Brazilian tourists who are in a big hurry."

Berta observed in admiration. "I can't help imagining this place, which all Bulgarians considered holy, under the reign of Sarah-Theodora, the Jewish queen who converted to Christianity. In 1350, Columbus hadn't been born yet, and of course America hadn't been discovered, but Bulgaria was already at the end of its second empire. There are so many graves with the names Hazan and Michael – our ancestors – in the cemeteries of Bulgaria's big cities. Even though we're Brazilian now and have no plans to come back here, there's nothing in the world that could weaken our ties to this country."

We stopped by the cemetery to pay our respects to our parents, grandparents, and my friend Salvator. We spent a small sum to have their graves cleaned and then went to Corecom, a store where everything was sold in dollars and where we opened an account in the name of David Hazan.

Then, it was time to say our goodbyes.

"Let's get this show on the road!" I said.

David said nothing in reply, but the look he gave me left no doubt whatsoever. Nothing would stop us now.

We went from Bulgaria to Spain. There, we stayed at Nissim's summer home in Guadarrama, a few miles outside Madrid. Maria Luiza took Berta, Daniel, and Sara on a quick tour of Toledo, where our ancestors had resided 500 years before, until they were expelled during the Inquisition. At least that's the way my grandfather had told the story.

"I don't know this Max Haim fellow personally, but I'm sure he knows what he's doing. A friend of mine assured me that he's already arranged the escapes of a number of people, and he's never had a plan go wrong," Nissim said between sips of wine.

Nissim had placed a few international calls, and an acquaintance had given him Max Haim's Vienna telephone number. We lost no time calling him, and to our good fortune, he picked up the phone. Nissim introduced himself and then said he had an important matter to discuss and would be willing to meet Haim anywhere. Nissim and I traveled to Vienna the next day.

We met Haim at a restaurant near the Stephansplatz, in the very heart of Vienna. He was a plump, hearty-looking gentleman who bore no resemblance to the James Bond character we figured we'd be meeting. I told him David's story and asked for his advice. Haim confirmed that he'd worked a few times for Simon Wiesenthal, the famous Nazi hunter, and that he'd also helped some people flee countries in the communist bloc. In his spare time, he ran a very well-known antique store in Vienna.

"This type of undertaking has to be very well-thought-out. It doesn't have anything to do with leaping the Berlin Wall or sprinting across the border," he said with a smile. "As you can see, I'm not built for any of that. In your case, the first thing to do is to wait for a response to the passport request. Then, we can lay out a plan."

"What are the odds of success if he needs to make a run for it?" I asked nervously.

"That depends on two things," Haim replied. "First, are you willing to invest about $40,000 in the project? The second question is whether your relatives can get permission to travel inside the Soviet bloc at least. It's usually easy to get authorization to visit Romania or East Germany, where the

Soviets have strict controls. If they manage to obtain this authorization, it'll make things easier, and we'll just need to wait till next summer. Your brother and his son will be here in Vienna in July 1974. I'm very happy to do this for free for people I like. I'm a survivor of the Mauthausen concentration camp, and I understand all too well what you're going through."

We agreed to leave the second plan as a backup and wait to see how the situation developed. I had no clue how an escape would actually be carried out, and I have to confess that it made me uneasy when Haim mentioned Romania and East Germany. On the other hand, I had to admit that our chubby James Bond seemed trustworthy and quite capable.

* * * * *

We went back to Manaus and to our work. We had to come up with at least $40,000, a huge amount back then. The export business was weak in 1973, but imports were going strong. We imported sizable orders of Pioneer tape decks for cars and stereos, different brands of radio recorders, electric knives, and hair dryers from Panama, none of which could be had on the Brazilian market. Berimex was also doing well, but we needed increasing amounts of capital. We opened our first car dealership at the close of the year, which meant more hard work. Right around then, our partner, Gustavo, came into an unexpected inheritance and offered to give the company a good injection of capital in exchange for a greater slice of the ownership pie. We didn't have much choice, so we took him up on the offer, and this financed the rapid growth of both Berimex and Amazon Flower.

With cash in our hands, business warmed up immediately. We learned that when you're on the mark with a business or product, you can expect a fast return on your money. On the other hand, mistakes bring bitter losses. When this is the case, you've got to be relentless in stopping the flow of blood: take the hit, tighten your belt, and get back to work.

Daniel started working at Amazon Flower and gradually assumed management of Berimex as well. He was a much better businessman than I ever was. After all, he'd been trained for it. I simply listened to my intuition and remembered my brief lessons from Leon Farhi. Sara wanted to keep studying. After graduating from Berkeley with a degree in Economics, she decided her real vocation was the law. This was a field she could study nowhere but in Brazil, so she moved back to Manaus, and our little family was together once again. David and Oleg were the only ones missing.

At the end of that year, David and Oleg were informed that their request to travel to Brazil had been refused. I knew that 1974 was going to be busy, so I told Max Haim that the only solution was to take the more radical path and that the money was available. One week later, Haim called to say that someone in our circle of trust would have to travel to Vienna to receive instructions as soon as possible, and then continue on to Bulgaria to pass the information along to David. We held a family meeting and decided Sara and I would go to Europe for as long as it would take.

From that point on, things happened very fast. When we arrived in Vienna, Max gave us a semi-professional camera and showed us what size and type of photos we were supposed to take of David and Oleg. Albert Göring immediately came to mind, and I suspected that the pictures were for fake passports. I pointed out to Max that David was very well known in Sofia and could be found out. Max laughed. "Don't worry, my friend. We're staging a military operation, and I'm being extremely cautious. Eventually you'll realize how seriously I'm taking everything. We've got two lives in our hands."

We decided Sara should travel to Bulgaria alone since

I'd attract more attention, and we needed to avoid that.

"What's even more important than the pictures of David and Oleg are their travel plans to Prague in late June. There'll be a quick stopover in Budapest, Hungary, and then they'll go back to Sofia around July 10," Max said, wasting no time. "Two layovers are essential for the greatest safety margin. Licco, you'll have to transfer some more money into David's account at Corecom so he's got enough. In early May, David and Oleg have to ask for authorization to take this little trip, all inside the Soviet bloc. You get a yes or no answer to this type of request almost immediately. Actually, you don't even need a passport, only the authorization. With that paper in hand, David has to buy the plane tickets." Max's expression grew even more serious. "Between May 25 and 30, very early in the morning, David will get three phone calls in a row, one right after another, but the caller won't say anything, just hang up. David should leave his room at 10 that morning and head to the downtown Corecom store, where he'll buy American cigarettes and some other little thing. On his way to or from the shop, a messenger will make contact with him, and David will give him all the essential information – travel dates, flight numbers, airline, schedule. Sara has to set all this up with David and Oleg. There's no room for uncertainty."

I wanted to ask some more questions, but Max cut the conversation short. "If everything goes as I hope, our man will return to Vienna with good news that same day, and we'll pop open a bottle of champagne. Then, I'll fill you in on the next step. One last thing: nothing about this in letters. From now on, all communication must be verbal. We can't take any chances."

I didn't tell Berta about Sara's trip. I knew it would make her very nervous, and although I thought the first part of the operation didn't present any real danger, I preferred to leave the nervousness to me. Besides, it would be hard to get a call through to Manaus, given that a number of operators had to be involved along the way. Regardless, Berta would be frantic if she didn't hear from us, so I hoped for Sara's quick return.

Sara returned three days later, thank goodness. When I met her at the airport, I could tell she'd been crying, so I gave her a hug. When we were alone in the rental car, she started recounting her story. Everything had gone smoothly with David and Oleg. They'd taken several photos, and Sara had passed the instructions along during a hike in the mountains. There'd even been time left over to see more of the city, in the company of Oleg. Winter is harsh in Bulgaria, and Sara had found Sofia much grayer than on her previous visit in May. Four hours before her flight was scheduled to take off for Vienna, she arrived at the airport and checked her bags. When she presented her passport at emigration control, she sensed something was wrong.

"Dad, nobody there spoke anything but Bulgarian. No English, no Spanish, no other language. Your brother and Oleg had already left. I finally figured out that the police were looking for that form you fill out when you get there. I tried to explain that the hotel had kept the piece of paper when I checked in, together with my passport. I'd actually tried to keep them from holding my passport hostage like that, but it didn't do any good. After I paid the bill and was about to step out of the hotel, they gave me back my passport – but the darn form stayed there. I didn't complain, because I thought it was the standard procedure. A half hour later, a grouchy agent who spoke English appeared. I repeated my story, and things just got worse." Sara's eyes were still filled with tears.

"The fellow called the hotel and talked with someone at reception for a good long while. The whole time he was on the line, he kept shaking his head no, and I began crying in despair. It seemed like it would never end. When he hung up, he didn't say a word, but just walked out of the room and left me waiting for almost another half hour. I remembered your friend Salvator and started picturing the fellow in all kinds of embarrassing situations. It's hard to believe, but it really helped! I don't know what happened, but the man suddenly reappeared, stamped my passport, and let me go. I got on the plane and then broke down sobbing. I was shaking all over, and I only felt better when we began our descent into Vienna. If I hadn't gotten to the Sofia Airport so early, I probably would have missed my flight. You'd have gone crazy if I hadn't gotten off that plane."

I was familiar with Bulgarian bureaucracy, and I could imagine how much my courageous daughter had suffered. At the same time, I had to suppress my amusement. "Sara, honey, I'm so sorry about what happened. Believe it or not, I'm somewhat to blame. I should have told you earlier that when you shake your head in Bulgaria, it means 'yes' and not 'no.' Don't ask me why, but Bulgarians are different from the rest of the world, even in this."

Sara stared at me in utter disbelief, and then her face lit up in a smile that showed off the dimples she'd inherited from Berta.

Max Haim's next instructions were clear: "You can return to Brazil. There won't be anything else to do for the next few months. I'll expect you back here in Vienna on May 25." I had the impression he was happy with the first part of the operation.

* * * * *

The following months were very tense. I'd phone Max every once in a while, and he'd always assure me that preparations were proceeding as expected. Time seemed to stand still, and the only things that alleviated our anxiety were work and books.

We'd grown more and more interested in Brazilian literature, which the rest of the world knows so little about. We'd read everything from Machado de Assis to Jorge Amado. Berta always thought Amado was a strong candidate for Brazil's first Nobel Prize. It's hard to name a writer more popular in his or her country than he was, which is especially impressive because Brazilians aren't big readers. Some of his characters evoke a delicate sensuality that mirrors the Brazilian soul, and yet are devoid of the thinly veiled pornography that many modern authors seem unable to resist. His books entertain and entice you, while they also awaken your imagination.

The free trade zone was growing fast in Manaus, which kept our import business strong. Free trade areas always attract people who are eager to do business and make their fortune, and it was to be expected that a certain number of hucksters would be among them. I remember one episode involving a respected Portuguese retailer, who owned several shops around town. He fell victim to a very curious scam. A small wholesaler who had just set up shop offered to sell him a big shipment of Gobelins tapestries at a very low price. Nobody in Manaus had experience with the product, so the Portuguese fellow wasn't eager to buy. Then the wholesaler offered him a small lot on consignment, no money up front, and the retailer agreed to give it a shot. He soon found that he was selling several of the items a day. This got him excited, so he put in a bigger order. Once again, he was very happy with the results. He contacted the wholesaler, but this time was told that there were only 4,000 of the hotcakes left in stock, and now he was only selling them for cash in hand. Since his price was so low and the product was flying off the shelves, he argued, he couldn't justify any other form of payment.

The retailer decided to make the purchase anyway and paid for it all up front. Much to his surprise, the tapestries quit selling. Not a single interested customer showed up. The deceitful wholesaler never admitted that it was a setup and that he'd sent his own employees around to buy the tapestries, day after day. Despite suspicions, nothing was ever proven, and the Portuguese shop owner had to take the loss.

There have always been dishonest people in the world,

but they never lasted long doing business in Manaus. It was a small market then, where everybody knew everybody else and news spread like wildfire. Honest dealers new to the market were at a disadvantage, because the presence of the scam artists made merchants leery of anyone they didn't know. It's amazing how some folks can work so hard and apply such astonishing creativity toward cheating others. If they'd put the same effort into an honest day's work, they'd come out much further ahead.

May arrived at last, and this time, Berta and I went to Europe. We reached Vienna a day before Max Haim's messenger was traveling to Bulgaria to get the information we needed.

"What if David's phone doesn't work?" Berta asked.

"His phone's going to work. I don't believe in negative thinking. But don't worry. There's a Plan B, just in case," Max replied, putting a quick end to the conversation.

Three long days later, the messenger returned in triumph. We were waiting anxiously for him at the airport. From a distance, his broad grin told us the plan was working.

"They'll fly to Prague on June 13 on Balkan Airlines, and on June 18, they go to Budapest on the Hungarian airline Malev," the messenger said as soon as he left the international area.

Max, who'd been quite tense, looked relieved. He was quick to say, "Let's have dinner together. I'm dieting as usual, but today we'll eat and drink to our fill. Your brother and nephew already have one foot in Vienna. Over dinner, I'll tell you what the next step is."

I was baffled. Getting out of Hungary and into the West was just as hard as getting out of Bulgaria. Why was Max celebrating as if the worst were behind us? We could scarcely wait for dinner.

"Let's analyze the situation," Max said that night.

We were seated at an elegant restaurant, almost next door to the Vienna opera house. A piano playing in the background contributed to the lovely ambiance.

"Inspired by this good music, and a few sips of wine, my assessment is that we're halfway there. We've got two good guys in Bulgaria who are packing their bags to take a trip. On June 13, they'll fly to Prague – which, by the way, is a gorgeous city. After a few pleasant days there, enjoying a little tourism and a lot of Pilsner, they'll catch a plane on Malev Airlines to Budapest. That'll be on the 18th. It'll be a short but vitally important trip, because it's during this flight that we'll pull the card out of our sleeve. So far, nothing unusual, right? Now comes the derring-do. A little before they get into Budapest, David and Oleg will discover that the nice Uruguayan couple sitting next to them actually knows them, and, in fact, has a gift for them."

"What do you have up your sleeve, fellow?" Berta asked skeptically. "Hijacking the plane?"

"Much to the contrary, Berta dear. I'm a peaceful man. The nice couple is going to hand the Bulgarian gentlemen two legitimate Uruguayan passports, with their own photographs and such in them, but with someone else's names. And the couple is going to keep David and Oleg's Bulgarian documents. Two Bulgarians and two Uruguayans will have boarded in Prague, but four Uruguayans and not one Bulgarian will get off in Budapest."

Max was bubbling over with enthusiasm about the plan. And we sat in stunned silence as he wove his imaginative tale. "To be on the safe side, the Uruguayan couple will go through passport control first, carrying the documents that could incriminate David and Oleg. Only then will our Bulgarians, disguised as Uruguayans, cross the border. All four will have legitimate stamps showing they entered Hungary. Once they've gone through customs, they'll join up with another four Uruguayans, who'll be waiting in the airport lobby. In the middle of the World Cup, a group of eight Uruguayan soccer fans will be traveling by van through Europe and will have to be in Germany the next day, where their team is going to play an important match. What the guards pay greatest attention to when you leave Hungary are your entrance stamps, which will be just as legitimate as the Uruguayan passports. The way you can check for a flaw is to shine a black light on the documents. We've done the test, and they passed with flying colors," he told us proudly. "At this time of year, especially during the World Cup, thousands of tourists flock to Prague and Budapest, and the group of Uruguayan fans won't even be noticed. The winds are all blowing in our favor right now. The road to Germany goes through Austria, and we'll be there to welcome our Uruguayan friends with open arms."

The way Max told the story, it all sounded very simple.

"So we needed false passports. Who was the counterfeiter? You?" I was dumbfounded.

"Look, Licco, first of all, I don't do that sort of thing. Second, I'd rather call the fellow who made the passports a craftsman or artist. Counterfeiter sounds so crude!"

"Kids," he went on, "You're on holiday for the next few days – a real vacation! But on June 17, we all have to be back in Vienna."

I suddenly felt calm and confident. I relaxed, pushed any misgivings aside, and saw that Berta had a confident smile on her face, one I hadn't seen in a long while. Dinner was excellent and the wine, even better.

"Now, I really believe that everything's going to turn out fine. I just don't know how we're going to stand the long wait until the big day!" I exclaimed.

Berta had a brilliant idea. "Why don't we go to Istanbul

for a few days? We can look up Omer, whom we haven't had any contact with for years. We can relive a bit of our courtship and our wedding. It's been 30 years…"

"Of course! We have such beautiful memories of Istanbul. Let's stay at that hotel near Istiklal Avenue and Taksim Square. Back then, it was the best in town. If I'm not mistaken, it's called the Pera Palace. A lot of passengers on the Orient Express used to stay there at the turn of the century. When we were there the first time, the thought actually flit through my mind that one day we'd return to that wonderful place as tourists, this time with legal documents and some money in our pockets."

The next day, we reserved our tickets to Turkey and included a quick stopover in Ephesus, where well-preserved ruins reveal a great deal about life in Ancient Greece and the Roman Empire. Berta had read about the Temple of Artemis, which was considered one of the wonders of the world in the first century B.C., when 250,000 people lived there. It was a once-in-a-lifetime opportunity to enjoy ourselves for a few days and educate ourselves a little about the history of the ancient world.

Although we couldn't shake our anxiety, it was a memorable trip. Omer, our host 30 years earlier, had passed away not long before, but we met his widow and his oldest son, who still ran the inn. It was moving to see the place again, changed so little by the years, a place that had been so important in our lives. Although we took up lodgings at the magnificent Pera Palace, we made it a point to spend one night at the inn that had given us shelter when we most needed it; it also had been the setting for our wedding. So during our nerve-wracking wait, we lived some moments of pure magic.

We went back to Vienna reinvigorated and found Max more optimistic than ever. We were so anxious that we stayed cooped up in our hotel room, reading and watching television while the minutes slowly crept by. Finally, at 2 in the morning on June 19, a van packed with noisy Uruguayan tourists pulled up in front of our hotel, bringing with it David and Oleg. The Uruguayans couldn't thank Max Haim enough for the trip he'd sponsored, and they continued on their way to Germany. Coincidentally or not, Uruguay's match would be against Bulgaria. Both sides were disappointed by the 1-1 tie. Like Brazil, the Uruguayans and Bulgarians went home early, driven off the field by Holland's Clockwork Orange. Twenty years later, Bulgaria, led by Hristo Stoichkov, would finish a historic fourth place in the 1994 World Cup, while Brazil would win its first title since the Pelé era, realizing its fervent dream of securing a fourth world championship.

Max Haim helped legalize David's and Oleg's status in Austria and aided them in making *aliyah* to Israel. My brother and nephew were the perfect example of a successful immigrant story; they humbly accepted the rules of immigrant life and wholeheartedly worked to adapt to their new home. Many people can never resign themselves to the differences between one country and another, and they futilely try to change certain things in their new homeland. That's always been a sure formula for failure.

Like many other young people, Oleg served in the Israeli Army. He learned Hebrew, got his degree in engineering, and, with the help of a rabbi, studied and converted to the Jewish faith. In keeping with his new religion, conversion was necessary even though his father was Jewish, because his mother wasn't.

David, ever faithful to his socialist ideals, opted to live on a *kibbutz*, where he met Ester, a very attractive young widow. They got married and had a son named Dov, 20 years younger than Oleg. My brother had a notable career in Israel and was the leader of his kibbutz for several years. He is no longer with us, may his memory be a blessing.

ILKO MINEV

The story of my nephew Oleg and brother, David, is so beautiful that to tell it, I'd have to write another account as long as this one. I'm afraid I don't have that much time left, and that's why I've decided to leave the task for Oleg.

CHAPTER XII

The bad with the good

Sara finished law school and got a job as a tax attorney, an area she understood well from her background in economics. When she was 28, she passed a civil service exam and became a judge with the Amazonas State Finance Court. In a few short years, she'd won the respect of her colleagues. There's a chronic shortage of good jurists in the Brazilian courts, in part because our legal system is one of the most complex in the world.

I've always felt that what Brazil needs more than sweeping tax reform is tax simplification. Everything is so complicated that businesses have to have internal departments that don't produce anything – their sole task is to make sure everything is in strict compliance with all the rules and regulations. Even so, it's easy for a business to slip up, make a mistake, and find itself accused of not complying with some rule, simply because the system is a minefield of convoluted regulations and myriad types of taxes. If a politician ever comes along with the will and determination to remedy the so-called "Brazil Cost" – the high operational cost of doing business in Brazil – and boost productivity, lower the tax burden on businesses, and reduce corruption, I suggest he or she begin by simplifying the tax system.

If you stop and think about it, it's a miracle that Brazil has managed to do so well for itself, despite a series of poorly structured economic plans, runaway inflation, frequent devaluations, economic stagnation, overwhelming foreign debt, and – as a consequence of all this – eight different currencies just in the time Berta and I have been in Brazil. When we first arrived, Brazil's money was called the Cruzeiro. In February 1967, it was replaced by the Cruzeiro Novo. Three years later, we were back to the Cruzeiro again. In February 1986, the Cruzado was introduced, and, then in January 1989, supplanted by the Cruzado Novo. The Cruzeiro was resuscitated in March 1990. The Cruzeiro Real was created in 1993, (comma) but it only stayed around until July 1994 with the introduction of the Real, (comma) which has endured as Brazil's currency ever since.

A large part of the blame for this economic chaos goes to the blundering administrations that have ruled the country since the early 1960s, military and civilian alike. The country didn't want to take the bitter orthodox medicine prescribed by the International Monetary Fund, resorting instead to home remedies that had no chance of working. Our economists were incredibly efficient at doing things that didn't need to be done. Another culprit behind the wretched state of the economy was petroleum and the fact that Brazil never handled any of its oil crises properly. Excessive government ownership, bureaucratic red tape, and the failure to invest in infrastructure delayed Brazil's development and hampered the fight against inflation, which strangled the country for more than 20 twenty years.

Facing inflation, it's no secret that the Brazilian government invented tax upon tax. The richest still managed to make money, while the poor grew poorer still. Given this twisted state of affairs, the average citizen and private enterprise, which, after all, pay the bulk of taxes, were always under the control of the government, while the ever-fattening public sector had free rein. For some historical reason, productive activities began to be treated not as vital generators of the wealth of the nation but as suspicious activities engaged in by individuals who were hungry for profit at any price. Growing ever bigger, the government never had enough funds to invest in infrastructure, security, or education. Even today, Brazilians have trouble recognizing that education is a far superior investment than the social programs we take such pride in, because education equalizes opportunities and is the most efficient way of distributing wealth. Only better education, greater infrastructure, and less bureaucracy can spare us from mediocrity.

Nonetheless, since the region where Berta and I lived was an exception, imports at Amazon Flower climbed substantially and brought us a high rate of return. Sometimes this justified not making any profit on our exports so we would have the right to a higher import quota. When Betamax and VHS video cassette players hit the market in the 1980s, Amazon Flower took full advantage. Around the same time, foreseeing a future real estate boom, we bought some of those weekend homes on the edge of town known as banhos. By then, their streams were no longer so clear, and the owners no longer wanted to escape the heat by spending their weekends there. We used our unexpected cash flow and the attractive prices of the banhos to build quite a solid portfolio of real estate investments.

Berimex flourished in those years of high inflation and economic stagnation in Brazil. It might seem absurd, but it's absolutely true: the richer not only figured out how to live with inflation but how to capitalize on it. They became experts in financial management and earned money without having to work at all. It was obvious that this warped speculative habit was very bad for the country. For instance, you had two chances to rake in profits on imports: once when you sold the product and once on the difference between the official exchange rate and the black market, which might be as much as 50 percent.

One day, I received a visit from a Japanese fellow who

represented a well-regarded VCR manufacturer. I asked him what his price was *FOB Panama.*

"One hundred dollars per one if you buy shipment of 400," he replied in fractured English.

I did my calculations and closed the deal.

"For how much you gonna to sell to clients?" he wanted to know. I told him I planned to charge the equivalent of 90 dollars in Cruzados on the black market.

"You gonna to lose money?" he asked, sounding somewhat dubious.

"No, sir! We're going to make at least 20 percent."

The Japanese gentleman raised his eyebrows. The harder I tried to explain, the less he understood. In fact, he was so mystified that he never did send us our order. The huge disparities between the official exchange rate and the black market yielded such absurd distortions that you could make big money without making much effort at all.

One perversely entertaining episode took place in the Manaus business world around 1980. A large number of counterfeit products were making their way into the country back then, especially watches and clothing apparel. It wasn't unusual for the naïve buyer of a Lacoste golf shirt to discover that his tiny alligator had disappeared in the first wash. Some wholesalers specialized in fake watches, including Rolex, Cartier, and Vacheron Constantin. These were a hot commodity, especially among the smugglers who habitually haunt free trade areas. One such importer received a shipment of 200 Cartier watches, but he didn't have much luck selling them on the Manaus market. He approached a retailer who was quite rude and called the watches "junk" – employing some more vulgar descriptors as well. Though his accusation was nothing but the honest truth, he didn't need to put it in those terms. Gossip has it that the impolite shop owner received a long-distance phone call the next day.

"Hello, this is Captain Garcia, with Vasp Airlines. Remember me? Have you got any Cartier watches in stock, wholesale?"

"Of course," came the answer. "How many do you need?"

"At least 300."

"I think I've got 180 or 200," the retailer replied, starting to drool.

Pilots and flight attendants who flew the Manaus route would often supplement their salaries by reselling schlock they bought in the free trade zone. The shop owner had no recollection whatsoever of any Captain Garcia, but he'd dealt with a lot of pilots. It usually meant good money for him.

"How much? Depending on the price, I'll take them all. I get in at noon tomorrow, and I'll go straight to your store. I'm only going to be in Manaus a few hours."

Lively negotiations followed, and the two men finally settled on a price. The pilot insisted on a certain kind of packaging, so that he and the flight attendants that were going to help him wouldn't attract any special attention from the airport agents.

Shortly after this conversation, the retailer rang the wholesaler who had offered him the Cartiers.

"Hey, buddy, have you still got those crappy watches?"

"I've sold some, but I must have around 150 left."

Another round of negotiations ensued, and the 150 watches were sold and paid for on the spot. The only thing that fell through the cracks was Captain Garcia, who never has shown up in Manaus. I don't need to say that both of those involved in the story (I'd rather not mention their names) were the brunt of countless jokes, and they never spoke to each other again.

* * * * *

One day, my friend Zanoni Magaldi stopped by the office. He wanted to discuss the idea of our going together to purchase a large lot on the edge of Maués River that had suffered significant environmental degradation. The land lay immediately adjacent to his property and extended along a beautiful beach. Berta, who loved the area, was quick to warm to the idea – especially because not much money was at stake. We closed the deal, and the next year built a small, cozy house there, with a lovely view of the beach. We hired one of Magaldi's former employees as caretaker and began planting a stand of rubber trees on our part of the property.

We would regularly spend a few days at a time in that magical place, and Sara and Daniel often went along. Looking back, those were the best years of our lives.

In 1977, our family grew when Sara married Sérgio, an old boyfriend. She was a 32-year-old woman by then, her career well underway, and she was ready to have a family and raise children. Sérgio, the nephew of my friend Moyses Bentes from Belém, was a prominent researcher at *INPA*, the National Institute for Research in the Amazon, as well as a biology professor at the Federal University of Amazonas.

Just a few months later, Daniel introduced us to his girlfriend, Rachel, the sister of one of Sara's childhood friends. The time had finally come for Berta and me to think about grandchildren and about cutting back on our workload.

We'd been going over possible dates for Daniel and Rachel's wedding when something happened that seemed minor at first. It was a Sunday morning, and I was just waking up. When I opened my eyes, I saw that Berta was examining herself carefully in front of the mirror.

"Licco, come here and help me," she said. "I found a little lump in my breast."

I put my finger on the spot and felt a tiny little something under her soft skin.

"It wasn't there yesterday," I teased her.

"I'm going to see Dr. Wallace. I'm sure it's nothing serious, but better safe than sorry."

Coincidentally, we ran into Dr. Wallace at the club later that morning, and Berta managed to get in to see him the next afternoon.

I could tell she was quite nervous when she got back from his office. "Licco, I'm thinking about going to São Paulo. The sooner, the better," she said.

"What's up, Berta? Tell me."

"Dr. Wallace ordered a lot of tests. He warned me that this little lump might be malignant. The chances are small, but they do exist. Especially since my mother died of cancer."

"It won't be anything, but let's not tempt fate. I'll buy us tickets for tomorrow. As they say, when it's something serious, there are only three good doctors in Manaus: Varig, Vasp, and Transbrasil. We'll go straight to Albert Einstein Hospital."

The biopsy detected a malignant tumor. Berta immediately had surgery on her right breast and then began chemotherapy. She was a compliant, courageous patient and, thank God, not one bit discouraged. For nearly a year, we flew back and forth between Manaus and São Paulo. Needless to say, I had my fill of airplanes and airports.

In the end, Berta's hair grew back rather quickly, and she was soon feeling better, so we decided to celebrate the conclusion of her chemotherapy at our house in Maués.

"How about we invite our friends to spend a few days with us?" Berta suggested, already excited about the idea.

"Fantastic, Berta! We can invite David and Oleg. I owe them the trip. We'll invite Nissim and Maria Luiza too, and maybe Saul and Eva Farhi from New York. None of them have been to the Amazon. And we can't forget Garry and Maria."

"Where are we going to find room for so many people? Our place is too small."

It was my turn to have an idea. "We can rent a boat with air-conditioned cabins and dock it at the beach in front of our house. Problem solved! We've got to invite the Bentes from Belém too, and Max Haim."

"Even better: what if we have Daniel and Rachel's wedding then too?"

"Good God, Berta! What will we do with the other guests? It's so inconvenient to get to Maués."

"Licco, I'm not talking about holding the ceremony in Maués. It'll be at the Tropical Hotel in Manaus. But this way our guests from abroad can be there too. After that, we can spend some days in Maués. Just think!"

"You're a genius, darling. If Daniel and Rachel agree, that's what we'll do."

Putting on lovely, lively parties is a Brazilian specialty; we're masters at the art. David, Ester, and Oleg flew in from Israel. Nissim came from Madrid by himself; his wife, Maria Luiza, wasn't in good health and was afraid of long flights, so she decided to stay home. Eva Farhi came from New York, along with her oldest son, Leon. Maria came from Louisiana; Góran, from São Paulo; and from Belém, our friends Moyses and Débora Bentes. We got a big surprise when we went to pick Nissim up at the airport: Max Haim, sporting a beard. We hadn't expected him, because a few weeks earlier he'd politely declined our invitation, explaining that he had prior commitments. Without saying anything to us about it, Nissim had insisted, and Max had eventually agreed to join him.

Only hours before the ceremony, Sara and Sérgio shared with us that she was expecting. Berta had endured the long trial of her disease without shedding a single tear, but this massive dose of happiness did her in. She cried without stopping for a good long while, first hugging me, then kissing Sara and Sérgio, and so on and so forth. We wallowed in complete, unparalleled happiness.

* * * * *

"Shabbat right on our boat," exclaimed Max. "Wonderful." He admired the table, with everything laid out. "It's hard to imagine this here, in the middle of the jungle."

We were all comfortably settled on the boat, which fittingly bore the indigenous name "Umuarama," meaning "place beneath the sun where friends gather." We would reach Maués the next day, where Berta had another surprise waiting for us: a torch-lit dinner on the beach in front of our house.

After our evening Shabbat meal on the deck, we sat enjoying a balmy, tropical night. Between one caipirinha cocktail and another, with good music in the background, we reminisced about the past. We had all survived a cruel era, and now we had more than enough reasons to celebrate.

"If I was ever poor, I don't remember it," Berta said, beaming with happiness.

That's exactly how we all felt at that magical moment. I knew how hard she'd work to put this together, from the wedding to the marvelous reunion with our friends.

Berta got up and changed records on the player. A husky female voice invaded the night: *Where have all the flowers gone...*

"Oh my God, 'Where Have All the Flowers Gone!'"

exclaimed Eva Farhi. "I haven't heard Marlene Dietrich in ages. Such a dramatic, sensual voice. She made this song popular all over the world, a regular anthem of resistance to cruel, pointless wars."

"In a way, as survivors of World War II, we're still searching for our lost flowers," Max said. "Thank goodness, all these many years later, the flowers have started blooming again."

No one said anything for a while, each of us absorbed in our memories. Then, I asked Berta to put on something a little more upbeat. She chose a Brazilian LP.

"It's amazing what a rich range of motifs and rhythms Brazilian music has," said Eva. In the U.S., we're only familiar with a few songs and a bit of samba. But here I've learned that samba is just one among many rhythms."

"We don't know much about Brazilian music in Europe either, but I think that's going to change very soon," Max affirmed.

In the 1980s, Brazilian music really was unknown outside Brazil. It exploded in subsequent decades, captivating audiences from France to Australia, from Canada to China. In its infinite variety, it is one of the finest expressions of Brazilian culture.

At Jewish social gatherings, it's quite common for the night to end in heated debate, each participant passionately defending his or her point of view. Our group looked to be no different. Nissim was an atheist, David a skeptic, I a moderate, Moyses a traditionalist, and Eva, orthodox. Nothing more natural than for religion to fuel a good discussion at Shabbat.

"Licco, did you know that Einstein, whom you love to quote so much, was really an atheist?" Nissim was bating me.

"That's not true." I said, defending my idol. "Much to

the contrary, he insisted that science without religion is lame, and that religion without science is blind."

Nissim pulled a piece of paper from his pocket and read: "The word 'god' is for me nothing more than the expression and product of human weakness, the Bible a collection of honorable but still purely primitive legends which are nevertheless pretty childish. No interpretation, no matter how subtle, can change this for me."

"That statement," I retorted, "comes from a letter Einstein wrote to a philosopher friend of his in 1954. The text is known as the 'God letter,' and it's a veritable heirloom among the great man's thinking."

Nissim shouldn't have meddled in such a volatile hornet's nest. He'd clearly armed himself for this debate, and now he was twisting things his way.

But Berta came to my rescue. "Einstein was never an atheist! He simply questioned the holy books, which many orthodox believers take as dogma. Einstein didn't go along with rigid interpretations, and he felt that words that had been written so many years ago reflected the cultural understandings of their time. He believed that the people who wrote them had their own limitations and that their target audience was even less educated. To keep people under control and protect them from disease and bad habits, the sages needed to describe a God who was both merciful and worthy of adoration, but at the same time authoritarian and fear-provoking. Our religion's dietary restrictions, for instance – we still follow them today – have a lot to do with sanitary concerns."

Eva was religious but also a scientist and a professor at Columbia University, and she was indignant. She cited Einstein once again: "'The more I study science, the more I believe in God.' He couldn't get any more explicit than that. He also said, 'I cannot conceive of a genuine scientist without profound faith' and 'I maintain that the cosmic religious feeling is the strongest and noblest motive for scientific research.'"

I breathed a sigh of relief. That was precisely the phrase I'd been trying to remember in response to Nissim's provocation. Eva was an unconditional fan of the great physicist and humanist, and she read everything published about him. Nissim had gotten himself caught in an argument he'd never win.

David brought the conversation to a close his way. "Maybe Einstein did doubt certain teachings. A wise man once said that doubt is one of the names of intelligence. Shabbat shalom, everyone!"

The next night, sitting on the beach around a big bonfire, we had another memorable discussion, this time regarding Israel's current position in the world. David and Oleg understood the topic well, but even they defended divergent opinions on occasion.

"Israel will eventually have to accept a Palestinian state," Moyses declared, igniting the controversy.

"Just after World War II, the U.N. voted in favor of creating the State of Israel," said Berta. "At the same time, it recommended that a state be created for the Arabs in the region. Back then, everyone there was Palestinian, Arab or Jewish. Well, we all know the history: the Arab countries didn't go along with that solution, and they almost destroyed Israel in the first few days of its existence. The problem isn't that Israel has to recognize their right to exist; to the contrary, they have to recognize Israel's."

"Exactly!" David spoke up. "Israel's stance is that everything should be discussed bilaterally, in direct negotiations, eyeball to eyeball. If they don't recognize Israel as a legitimate state, we won't negotiate. How can you engage in dialogue with someone who wants to destroy you?" David concluded.

I asked Oleg's opinion. As a veteran who had been on

active duty, he knew more than we did about the State of Israel's official position.

"There's a consensus within the government now that Palestine will exist one day," he stated categorically. "Rabin and Peres are ready to negotiate with Arafat. The question is whether Arafat speaks for Palestinians or not. If the Palestinians and the Arab nations do not officially recognize Israel, there will be no talks and no peace. It might take 20, 30, or 50 years to finish negotiations, but I believe common sense will prevail in the end," Oleg predicted. "In the meanwhile, there will continue to be clashes, and Israel has to win all the battles and all the wars. We know that if we lose just one, we'll be wiped off the map. World opinion doesn't take this into account, and even some of our allies pressure us to negotiate a shaky peace. But if such a peace didn't work out, I don't know whom they'd offer their condolences to, because we'd all be dead. It's simple: we won't give in on this point."

Max chimed in. "If the Palestinians put down their weapons, negotiations will take place, and a peace settlement will eventually be reached. If Israel puts down its weapons, what we'll see the very next instant is the greatest holocaust in modern history, and Israel will be wiped off the map. This destruction is the raison d'être of a number of organizations and nations." He was incensed. "There's not a single country in the world that would negotiate with an enemy under these terms. It's regrettable that even some countries that are Israel's friends – brimming with good will but ignorant of the facts and lacking a clear perception of the danger – insist that we have to be more trusting of our adversaries, even without any guarantees. It's not their hides that are at stake," Max said in conclusion.

On our way back to Manaus, we had another dinner aboard the Umuarama and, as you might expect, another debate. It was only the subject matter that changed, while the fervor of the discussions was the same as always. The second time around, the big topic was international pressure on Brazil, which had failed to control the burn-offs occurring in vast areas of the Amazon. In the states of Pará and Rondônia and the territory of Acre, agricultural and livestock-raising activities were advancing swiftly, straight into the forests. The traditional method for clearing large areas of land for grazing cattle was to indiscriminately burn off vegetation. New technological resources, including satellite images, left no room for doubt: the great rainforest was under brutal attack. While there were some grounds for the international reaction, it was also quite overblown. It was as if Brazil – and not the more industrialized nations – were the prime culprit behind global warming.

Berta and I contained ourselves at first but to our surprise, arguing our side proved easier than we thought. Clever as always, Berta posed the right question: "How many burn-offs have you seen on this trip? Not one! Zero! The only fire you've seen was from our beachside barbecue pit. There's no doubt that we've got a serious problem in other regions, but in any case, the damage being done by developed nations is much greater. In the state of Amazonas, where most of the Amazon rainforest lies, there are no large burn-offs. And oversight is increasing elsewhere around the country and becoming more effective too."

Then David asked a question we didn't know how to answer. "How many forest rangers work actively in the Amazon? If you don't have well-trained rangers and good intelligence, it's really hard to do conservation work. A short while back, I read that the tiny country of Finland has more forest rangers than all of Brazil. The local residents who live scattered across the gigantic Amazon could easily play this role. It would be a way to create jobs in the interior in exchange for a vital service."

"It's not that simple," I protested. But since I didn't have any more arguments, I changed the subject.

Despite these disagreements, our days in Maués were absolutely delightful. Manoel, our caretaker, and Jacira, his wife, spared no effort to make sure we had everything we needed. Our friend Zanoni also helped in his own way by providing us with a range of fish for our meals – tambaqui and pirarucu. We also used his canoes to fish for peacock bass in nearby lakes. For years after, our friends who had been with us reminisced about that unforgettable excursion and regaled their families with stories about the wonders of Maués. David returned to Manaus other times, and Oleg actually moved to the Amazon not long after. We went to Maués again in the company of friends, but I never again managed to gather together so many loved ones, and no other trip, no matter how enjoyable, has ever compared to those magical days.

On the last day of our journey, just hours before we caught sight of Manaus, Oleg said he wanted to talk to us. In Bulgarian, he asked, "Aunt Berta and Uncle Licco, that invitation of yours, from 10 years ago in Vienna, to come live in Brazil – does that still stand?"

"Of course!" I replied. "That way, your dad would come visit us more often. There'd be plenty for you to do here. Our children would love it! You'd be more than welcome."

It took nearly a year to get a permanent resident visa for Oleg. Brazil doesn't exactly have its arms opened wide to new immigrants, even when they boast excellent credentials and already have work contacts. But, as usual, there's no hurdle that can't be overcome by a good "*despachante*" in Brasília – an expediter who cuts through red tape and greases the gears of bureaucracy.

* * * * *

Berta had the chance to know her first two grandchildren: Sara's daughter, little Berta, and Daniel's Ilana. However, a few short months after the wedding, during a routine exam, the doctors discovered another lump, this time in her left breast. It was as if the sky had fallen in on us. Our crucible began again.

We fought with every weapon at our disposal, and Berta maintained her tremendous spiritual strength. But in early 1985, the doctors at the hospital called me in to confirm my greatest fear: the disease was winning. Berta only had months to live. It was hard to believe, because although the treatment had weakened Berta, she was leading a practically normal life. We continued to pay frequent visits to our friends, and our home was always filled with them. She'd quit playing tennis a while earlier, and I knew she was saddened and discouraged by that. If she was in pain, she never let it show and never complained about anything. She was still working every day and was the same practical woman as always. Remarkably calm and collected, and over our protests, she transferred all her stock to our children and the real estate to me. Even ill, Berta was amazing. She hired Terezinha, a new cook. I could clearly see she was worried about how the house would be taken care of once she was no longer with us.

"Licco darling, I'd really like you to help me keep an interest in Bulgaria alive in Daniel and Sara. They speak a bit of Bulgarian, but they're completely illiterate in the language," she said with a smile. "We must never forget that it was Bulgaria that saved us 40 years ago. Our ancestors lived in that land and were happy there for 500 years, and that's where so many Michaels and Hazans lie buried. And we've got countless friends still living there. I'd really like our children and grandchildren to preserve this bond – a bond that's left such a deep mark on us."

I could tell this was extremely important to her, and I agreed without reservation. This was one of the things that convinced me to write this story.

We stayed strong during those months. We couldn't break down now that Sara had little Berta to care for and Raquel was expecting her first child. The world kept right on turning. After all, we were only visitors here. Although it was evident that Berta was getting everything ready for when she was gone, we never spoke of death.

On the eve of our 42nd wedding anniversary, in early December 1985, little Ilana was born. The next day, I sat down to write a letter to David, sharing the good news. Berta was in her favorite armchair reading a novel by James A. Michener, her preferred author right then. "Licco honey," she said, "The air conditioning is blowing right on your back. You're going to catch cold."

I changed positions and kept on writing. When I turned around a short while later, I saw that her book was lying in her lap, and I realized that my Berta was no longer with me.

It took me years to get used to her absence. She was an extension of my own body. Ever since Istanbul, we'd rarely been apart for more than a few days. The same pain I'd felt when I'd learned that Salvator was dead tormented me for a very long while, this time even stronger. I gradually withdrew from my business and transferred almost all my stock to Sara and Daniel. I was still strong of body, but losing Berta had left me vulnerable and depressed. I sought refuge in travel. I went around the world, to India and Nepal, then to South Africa and Kenya. I visited much of South and North America. I led a comfortable life, but a lonely one.

* * * * *

Amazon Flower exported rosewood and copaiba, but business started suffering when Brazil's environmental protection agency, *IBAMA*, imposed new restrictions meant to protect endangered species. Rosewood had gotten scarce in recent years, providing environmentalists with a legitimate concern. Under these circumstances, Zanoni started his first rosewood plantation in 1989. He was following the recommendation of his friend and client Samuel Benchimol, who said rosewood would be better than rubber trees, which were terribly prone to pests. This was so true that no one had ever successfully raised rubber trees in the Amazon for commercial purposes. It would be worth giving rosewood a try.

Not long after Zanoni got his project underway, I started a small stand of rosewood myself. It wasn't easy to get the seeds and saplings, but luckily enough, a community of caboclos on the Paracuni River agreed to help. They'd tried their best to come up with an economic activity that would guarantee their small village a stable income. As jobs related to the harvesting of natural products vanished, the caboclos had grown so desperate for work that for a short time they'd even assisted drug dealers who were secretly raising marijuana in the forest. The fields were discovered, and the community's leader subsequently spent a few days in the Maués jail. Since it was never proven that the community had taken part in any criminal activity, the leader was released. He then got in touch with Zanoni Magaldi, who had formerly bought copaiba balsam from the community. When Zanoni discovered that the caboclos could provide him with seeds and even some saplings, he wasted no time proposing a partnership.

So our fields got a big boost, the small community found itself a lawful economic activity, and the caboclos themselves planted a few hundred trees on their own land along the Paracuni. Zanoni managed to plant 400 trees the first year, while I put almost 100 in the ground. Our rosewoods grew well the following years, and we started to feel confident that our rather improvised enterprise would eventually yield fruit.

Then one fine day, I was contacted by a scientist from the University of Campinas in the state of São Paulo: professor Lauro Barata, an eminent authority in the field of rosewood essential oil. He spent a few weeks in Maués, where he made a brilliant proposal. Rather than cutting the planted trees, he recommended we should merely prune them and extract oil from their branches and leaves. The professor's work was fundamental in improving our procedures. We enhanced seed selection, ascertained the ideal distance between planted trees, and made the distillation process more efficient. Even though this new endeavor wasn't at all profitable, I'd stumbled upon something that was great for me. For the first time since Berta's death, I had something enjoyable to do, something that made me happy.

Around the same time, Oleg decided to get into the mining business. He had picked up Portuguese with ease and assumed management of the Berimex department that sold to *garimpos* on the Madeira River in Rondônia. These small gold mining operations were largely informal and sometimes even illegal. Much to my chagrin, Oleg was contaminated by the thirst for filthy lucre, like so many other people I've known. He used his savings to buy a *river-mining dredge* in one of the most promising areas along the Madeira – and one of the most dangerous as well. I tried my best to persuade him to walk away from this perilous pursuit, but he was as obstinate as his father.

Fortunately, Oleg never abandoned his principles, or his sobriety, during the two years he lived and worked in this strange world, populated by a gamut of characters – some decent, trustworthy friends and others who represented the dregs of the earth. I feared the worst and felt guilty, because I was the one who had introduced him to river mining, and in part that's why I went to visit him several times. Around 1988, the accumulation of floating dredges packed along the riverbanks were magnets for men in search of gold as well as for drugs, prostitution, and adventure. It was a hotbed for disease, violence, and death. In the midst of this mayhem, I actually met some of the dearest, most honest people I've ever known, but I also saw, in horror, how hundreds of lives and dreams were drowned in the roiling, muddy waters of the Madeira. I had experienced war, destruction, labor camps, and human misery, yet I suffered greatly when Oleg, of his own free will, risked his young life in that hostile environment.

ILKO MINEV

I only recently learned of the so-called War of Prainha, when a number of dredges that had enjoyed a run of especially productive days (Oleg's among them) were surreptitiously surrounded one afternoon in preparation for what was to be a surprise attack by hired guns that night. Luckily, Oleg noticed the canoes of strangers casually moving into strategic positions around the dredges. Recognizing an ambush in the making, Oleg mustered the skills and experience he'd acquired while in the Israeli Army and led a resounding counterattack, which earned him much respect and admiration among the majority of the miners. It was just as well that I was kept in the dark about the episode back then.

On a routine visit to Porto Velho, the capital of Rondônia, Oleg met Alice, a skinny girl of Jewish heritage who worked in the administrative offices of the new state. She'd been born in the rubber harvesting region of the Abunã River, on the border with Bolivia, where her great-grandfather had been a rubber baron years before. The story of her family was one of those unbelievable odysseys of the settlement of the Amazon that rivals fantasy and challenges our imagination. When she was just a teen, her parents and only brother succumbed to yellow fever, endemic in the region. Alone in the world, Alice had luck on her side. A woman living next door had taken her to the wife of the legendary "coronel" Jorge Teixeira, the last governor of the territory of Rondônia and its first governor after it earned statehood in 1981. The family took her in, protected her, and helped her through high school.

In those years, Brazil's youngest state needed all kinds of civil servants, so Alice was hired by the youngest state in the country right after her graduation. When Oleg met her, Alice was a determined young woman with a clear idea of what she wanted in life. Despite her frail demeanor, she was spiritually strong, very pretty, and cheerful by nature – like Berta when she was young. What neither I nor my brother, David, had managed to do – convince Oleg to give up mining – this charming girl accomplished in the name of love. Oleg wanted to be with her no matter what, and he wasn't about to run the risk of losing her. Alice loved Oleg too, and she wanted distance between him and the insecurity and violence of mining. Thus, the dredge was sold, and there was even a little gold left over, enough for the happy couple to start a life in the city of Porto Velho, where new opportunities were unfolding for anyone who wanted to work.

Even though many years have passed, I wish Oleg would tell his story one day – his story and the story of Rondônia and the Madeira River gold mines, which he knew so intimately. I know he's a talented writer, and I still hold out hope that these memories won't be lost to time.

CHAPTER XIII

Our new world

Tempora mutantur, nos et mutamur in illis
(Times change and we change with them)

The late 1980s saw a period of turmoil in Eastern Europe, with the Soviet giant in its death throes. Although Secretary-General Mikhail Gorbachev, supreme leader of the USSR, attempted to modernize the Soviet model by introducing Glasnost and Perestroika, his efforts proved useless. After decades of foolhardy practices, the communist economic model had worn out, and the unthinkable happened: complete collapse.

The events took me – like everyone else – by surprise. In hindsight, I can see that the symptoms of this collapse had been there for a long time, especially during the regime's last few decades. But at the time, nobody picked up on those signs or interpreted them properly.

The Soviet Union wasn't defeated by Western cannons or missiles; it crumbled under the pressure of economic disaster. In addition, the powerful empire was bombarded by a different and very unusual kind of weapon, unprecedented until then: the spontaneous, innovative music of the Beatles and Elvis Presley, Hollywood movies (not always grade A, but entertaining nonetheless), the advanced technology and designs of the automotive industry, the glamour of the cutting-edge fashion world, irresistible consumer goods, and freedom of expression and choice – in other words, the good things in life. Nothing could resist this powerful form of seduction; not the Red Army, the Berlin Wall, the KGB, nor the Communist Party's Politburo.

In 1985, the military dictatorship in Brazil finally came to an end. The transition to democracy was peaceful but nonetheless traumatic. Fate made the process more painful, as Tancredo Neves, the first civilian president elected after more than 20 years of an authoritarian regime, died unexpectedly before taking office. The country's fledgling democratic institutions were feeble at first but gradually gained muscle. These changes aside, Brazil's political life was still unsettled and bore the imprint of past vices. The new constitution of 1988 was a major step forward, shortcomings notwithstanding (period). Its defining of interest rates and other such matters, for example, was certainly inappropriate to include in a nation's charter.

Politics in Brazil continued to lack substance, while abounding in promises and grandstanding, not to mention endemic corruption. Despite it all, in fits and starts, our country was moving forward, and so were we. Although we lived in an imperfect society hooked on certain bad habits, we remained optimists. Distracted by the country's new victories on the soccer field and racetrack – the latter thanks to national hero Ayrton Senna – Brazil promised to be better in the future. It was a shame Berta didn't live to witness either the toppling of the Berlin Wall or Brazil's return to democracy.

In 1990, we managed to plant more rosewood trees than the previous year, which kept me in Maués for a good stretch of time. I let our caretaker, Manoel, have a vacation after the heavy work he'd done with the planting – and he could expect to have even more work looking after the young trees. At Berta's insistence, we'd built a small but comfortable brick home for him and his family behind our house. That way, they were nearby, but we still had our privacy.

Since it was Manoel's dream to visit Fortaleza, his father's hometown, where some cousins of his lived, I decided to give the whole family a bonus. I bought tickets for him, his wife, and his two daughters, and they took off on their first plane ride. Berta had really liked them. Whenever she could, she helped Jacira out, and sometimes she'd go over the girls' homework with them. In return, they not only took care of our farm and house, but they also cooked and did the laundry. The arrangement had worked to everyone's satisfaction for years, and it was a pleasure for me to be able to give them the trip in recognition of so much work well done. There's no way I could have foreseen that what promised to be a happy, relaxing event would end in tragedy.

Once they arrived in Ceará, a cousin drove the family to Morro Branco, a beach not far from Fortaleza. They spent the day swimming in the ocean, eating crab and fried fish on the beach, and savoring a beer or two. They headed back to Fortaleza late in the day. On the narrow road, their cousin must have fallen asleep at the wheel, because, for no apparent reason, he hit a bus head-on with his old station wagon, going full speed. The consequences were tragic. Everyone died instantly, except Laura, their oldest daughter, who by some miracle walked away with only minor contusions. Just 19 years old, she remained in a state of shock for days, while we had the bodies transported from Fortaleza to Maués and made funeral arrangements. It was traumatic for everyone involved.

After several days had passed, I started looking for a new caretaker, though I felt a bit awkward about it. After I hired one of the caboclos who had helped Manoel on several occasions and was familiar with the job, Laura came to talk to me. "Uncle Licco," she started, addressing me with the honorific she'd used since childhood. "I know I've got to move out for the new caretaker to move in. I'll be starting a job as an elementary school teacher this next year here in town. My parents, may they rest in peace, didn't leave me anything, and I can't afford to rent a place for myself yet. I don't know what to do, Uncle Licco."

Her voice choked up, and I could only imagine her pain.

"Laura, I'm in no rush. Why don't you let the new caretaker move in, and you can stay in one of the bedrooms of the main house as long as you need. Next week, I'm off to Manaus and then to Europe, and you can take care of the house while I'm gone. Your parents were always very devoted to us, and I'm very grateful to them. You're almost a daughter to me."

I could sense her relief. The poor child was alone in the world, still suffering profoundly from the untimely loss of her parents and sister. For my part, I'd be as helpful as I could.

My trip would take me to Bulgaria together with David, but I went to visit him in Israel first. I was awestruck by the country's rapid development. There was a striking difference between it and its neighbors. The green lands of Israel stretch to its borders. On the other side, the sterile colors of the desert prevail, and you rarely see any vegetation.

"We're growing and developing very quickly," David said proudly.

"I can tell. Growth means you're getting bigger, and development means you're getting better. You can feel both things happening here. Congratulations!"

David had just gotten news that he'd been "rehabilitated" by the new Bulgarian government and had received a formal apology for the judicial error. His friend Nikolai Chernev, whom I'd met in Mexico City 20 years before, had contacted him and would be waiting for us in Sofia.

We spent three weeks in Bulgaria, traveling the whole country in a rental car. We of course wanted to visit Somovit, where I spent nearly two years in a labor camp. It was no easy task locating the spot where our barracks had stood, because everything had changed. The road we were forced to work on had actually never been finished, and the barracks were no longer there. We visited some families who lived in the region, but no one remembered much about the labor camps. Their memories had faded so much that they couldn't comprehend the excitement of the two curious old visitors who had appeared out of nowhere.

Back in Sofia, we also tried to locate descendants of Mr. Denev, the fellow who had been Albert Göring's right-hand man and helped Berta, Nissim, and me escape from Bulgaria in 1943. We were lucky enough to track down one of Denev's children, who was trying to set up a small import business, as the market had recently opened up. We were surprised that he was aware of the events of 50 years earlier and the clandestine activities of his father with Albert Göring.

Since Mr. Denev had been extremely discreet, we couldn't find anyone else who was aware of the facts. We were informed that he'd died in anonymity in 1970 and that his other child, a political dissident, had managed to flee to the West shortly after his father's passing. I was happy to have located at least one person to whom I could express my gratitude before time erased the last shreds of memory.

Our dinner with Nikolai was an emotional moment for me. I knew him only from those brief moments in that Mexican hotel room. He'd lost status after the fall of the communist government and had retired, but he was happy.

"I couldn't stand the never-ending pretense and the lies anymore. I was an idealist in my youth, like David," he went on. "I hated the followers of Hitler and their Bulgarian lackeys. I was willing to die for my ideals. Then things changed. When

I met you in Mexico, Licco, I already had a wife and children, and, I have to admit, I was much less daring."

"No, you weren't a bit daring!" I ribbed him, and he had to agree.

It was Nikolai who advised us that we could ask for a copy of our dossiers from the time of the communist dictatorship. He also warned that David would probably uncover documents he didn't even suspect existed. It had been common for neighbors, friends, and colleagues to act as stool pigeons and to slander others just to get in good with some party member or avoid persecution by the security forces. I wasn't interested, but David insisted on filing a request for his dossier. With the help of friends, he got access almost immediately and then spent the day reading the stack of papers. When I met him for dinner later, I could tell that something was wrong.

"What's up, brother? Did you figure out the identity of the guardian angel who wrote reports about you for the security organs?" I asked in concern.

David looked me straight in the eye with that sorrowful expression, the image of our father, and said in a hoarse voice, "In the last year of marriage, even Irina. I'm not going to tell Oleg."

On my way back to Brazil, I spent two days in Grasse calling on my rosewood clients. They were all worried, because Brazil's environmental protection agency was progressively lowering the amount of wood that could be legally harvested, and availability was therefore on the decline. I explained that we couldn't exploit wild trees as before but that some production would continue, albeit trending downward. The alternative was to rely on the oil extracted from the branches and leaves of the few groves of planted trees. A number of manufacturers came right out and said they'd eliminate our product from their formulas if supplies didn't improve. It was indeed true that we hadn't been able to guarantee enough production lately to ensure regular supply. Not much oil was being sourced from branches and leaves yet, but with good organization and enough incentive, things could grow measurably. We had to convince government authorities to support those who wanted to plant. Manufacturers in Europe, the U.S., and Japan wanted our product. The only thing left to do was to organize sustainable production. In a few years, we could supply the world market, reap good rewards, and create more jobs for our caboclos.

I returned to Brazil optimistic, but unfortunately the feeling didn't last long. I soon discovered that Brazil's bureaucratic red tape, now under the guise of environmental concern, wasn't taking any type of productive activity into account. Many of the agencies that had the word "sustainable" in their names or bylaws actually cared very little about economic activities. Anyone who wanted to engage in business had to have various environmental permits from a slew of federal, state, and municipal agencies, from the Ministry of Culture, the Ministry of Agriculture, and God knows where else. And since they competed among themselves, these agencies often made conflicting demands.

Just as with taxes, the prime concern in the environmental realm should be to simplify and use common sense. The caboclos on the Paracuni River who planted rosewood instead of marijuana in 1990 understood this all too well: in order to prune the planted trees and produce oil, they had to file a project that included the deed to their land (along with other requirements). But since caboclos don't have access to Brazil's system of notary public offices and such deeds rarely exist in the remote interior of Amazonas, the trees weren't pruned, the caboclos had no work, and the false environmentalists patted themselves on the back for a job well done.

The last catch-22 they've invented is something called a Permanent Preservation Area, a concept that applies to all lands bordering rivers, which is where so many caboclos live and work. I'm sure the way these preservation areas were envisioned in 2012 must make sense somewhere, but not in the Amazon, where it's not easy to find places that don't lie near some watercourse. Any economic activity that occurs within this mind-bogglingly large space is subject to prior authorization from some bureaucrat who sits in an air-conditioned office several hours away by plane. It looks good on paper but is impracticable no matter how well intentioned, and it just ends up serving as a major incentive for raising marijuana, which, for obvious reasons, gets planted far away from the visible riverbanks. So much for sustainability.

CHAPTER XIV

The farm

Back in Maués, I continued my labors planting rosewood trees. Zanoni, Lauro Barata, and I conducted a number of successful experiments, pruning the trees different ways. We discovered that it took four or five years for them to be ready for pruning and that regrowth was vigorous. All indications were that it was a viable business. We had a long way to go, but we were headed in the right direction.

After Laura started teaching at the public school in town, she could afford rent, but I suggested she stay on at the farm anyway. It was very close to town, and she could bike to work in a few short minutes. Our deal was that instead of paying rent, she'd take care of the house and cook whenever I was in Maués. It was a good arrangement for both of us.

I'd spend my days at the nursery, getting new saplings ready, and I had hardly any time to chat with the few helpers I'd hired. I'd talk a bit with Laura at night; she'd tell me about her day, and I'd tell her about mine. Then, she'd prepare her classes, and I'd read my books or watch television. I grew so accustomed to having her around that I'd get especially lonely at my home in Manaus. The need to raise more seedlings and plant more trees was just an excuse to spend added time in

Maués, and it wasn't long before I realized that what I really liked was Laura's company and our conversations over dinner. I have to confess that it did flit through my mind that if I were 20 years younger, I'd have shown interest in things beyond mere chit-chat with that pretty young woman. Those were the thoughts of a 71-year-old man who would never have considered behaving disrespectfully toward a woman 50 years his junior, a woman who could have been his granddaughter.

Another year of hard work went by, and at the close of 1991, I tallied my planted trees at 1,500. It wasn't a lot, but it was a good start. While some rosewood was still being produced from trees felled in the forest, it was getting increasingly difficult to obtain the needed permits. There were a lot of dishonest folks in the business, and oversight had to be especially intense. On the other hand, the cost of doing inspections related to forest management plans was too steep for the slim budgets of government agencies, making the most practicable solution the outright prohibition of these activities.

In May 1992, I awoke with all the symptoms of malaria. It was the second time I'd come down with the disease, and I was all too aware of the suffering I was about to endure. But this time around, my case was much more severe. I had a terrible headache, a fever of 104, nausea, and chills in the late afternoons. I was familiar with these symptoms, but this time around, I also had violent chills, followed by hot flashes and profuse sweating. Periodically, I would lose consciousness or become delirious; then, I'd see jumbled visions from my youth, the labor camp in Somovit, and even my friend Salvator aboard the ill-fated *Jamaïque*, where he'd never set foot. There weren't many doctors in Maués in those days, but every one of them was all too familiar with malaria.

"A very severe case of malaria, but thank God it's benign," declared the young doctor who paid a house call. He prescribed quinine and some other medications. He also drew a blood sample, recommended complete bed rest, and I heard him ask Laura to contact him if her father hadn't improved within three days. As wretched as I felt, I still managed to find that humorous.

If you've never had malaria, it'll be hard for you to understand what I went through. Worse than the unbelievable cold were the tremors, which caused chest pain and went on and on as if they'd never stop. No matter how many blankets Laura put on top of me, the cold wouldn't go away. My teeth chattered until I was exhausted, and then I'd go back to my delirium.

When I woke up on the second morning, well before dawn, I saw that Laura had fallen asleep in a chair next to my bed. I stared at her face, relaxed in deep sleep, and I was overcome by a feeling of great tenderness for that devoted young girl. There was no denying that she had some Indian blood, thus her somewhat slanted eyes and black hair, long and straight. "The mixing of the races always produces such attractive features," I thought.

Right then, she woke up. When she noticed I was looking at her, she smiled.

"My gosh," she said, "I thought this night would never end! Now that the drugs have kicked in, the danger has passed."

That's when I realized I was wearing a different pair of pajamas than the ones I'd had on the night before. "Good God! She must have changed my clothes during the night," I said to myself in disbelief. I'd never felt so embarrassed.

Laura clearly guessed my thoughts. "You were drenched in sweat. I had to do it."

I felt better, though very weak, all day. But it started all over again later on. The high fever, nausea, cold, chills, violent tremors, delirium – it was sheer hell. When I came around in the middle of the night, I smelled a female aroma, delicious and unmistakable. I held my breath when I saw that Laura was sleeping right alongside me, her arms wrapped around me. It seemed like she wanted to protect me from the endless freezing cold. I didn't budge a muscle for a long time, because I didn't want to interrupt that beautiful sight. And I was surprised to find myself feeling things I hadn't felt in many ages. "Life is so unfair," I said to myself. "It robs us of our strength, but desire stays with us." I was so tired that I fell asleep again. When I awoke again, Laura was still lying next to me, but on top of the blanket now.

"I'm sorry. I didn't want to leave you alone, and I slept a bit right here," she said.

"You don't have to apologize, Laura. I'm really the one who should apologize for not letting you get a decent night's sleep. At least this time you didn't have to change my pajamas," I said, ashamed.

"You sweat less. But I think you had nightmares again."

The third day, it was the same thing all over: after feeling quite decent for several hours, my fever returned at the usual time, and with it, all my other miseries. But my symptoms didn't hit me as hard that day. I didn't become delirious, and I awoke in the middle of the night to Laura's rhythmic breathing in my ear. My fever had broken. I felt a strange peace come over me, and, still sleepy, I turned toward Laura and fell back to sleep.

I woke with the first rays of the sun and saw Laura's face up close to mine. She was motionless, staring at me, and when she saw I was awake, she said, "You were sleeping so nice! I think you're recovering well. You'll be able to go back to work real, real soon."

I spent the day in a state of confusion. The truth of it was, I hadn't had relations with a woman in a very long time, and the last two nights had left me with an odd feeling of happiness. What was happening? Was this physical proximity with Laura just a meaningless little thing? Or was there more to it? How could a 20-year-old girl be at all attracted to an old man like me? Deep inside, I knew things were headed in a dangerous direction and that I should be very careful. "Foolish behavior is one thing at the age of 20, but at 70, it's unthinkable," I thought. I had a duty to behave responsibly toward Laura, and toward my own family.

The fourth night was much better. The fever struck, but not the shakes. I slept well. I felt Laura lie down beside me, on top of the blanket again. We had a tranquil night, and when I woke up in the morning, she wasn't in the room. The doctor paid a visit that day. He was pleased with what he saw and recommended that I take it easy for another week. I wasn't completely over it, but I could leave the house and oversee work at the farm.

I hadn't said anything to my children about the malaria, in part because they wouldn't have been able to do anything anyway, except worry. Once the danger had passed, I went to the post office, where I could phone Sara. Her reaction was pretty much what I'd expected. "Dad, come back to Manaus now. They've got the best malaria specialists in Brazil at Alfredo da Mata Hospital. At your age, you shouldn't take any chances. You could have serious lasting consequences. You're not a kid anymore!"

I knew that, and I didn't need to be reminded so harshly. I promised I'd come home soon, and I went back to the farm before the time my fever always hit. That night, I told Laura I'd spoken with my daughter, and she replied with conviction, "Your kids'll be here to get you right away. I'm going to miss you."

Daniel did, in fact, show up the next day in a small twin-engine plane that he'd chartered. I gathered my things and went to say goodbye to Laura.

"I wish you all the best, Uncle Licco. I'll be here waiting for your next visit."

I don't know why she insisted on calling me "uncle" that time. I thanked her for everything she'd done and gave her a big smile. "I'm fine now, and I need to present myself to my family."

A few days later, Laura rang from Maués to inquire about my health, and we chatted a bit.

"Will you be coming back to Maués?" she asked.

"Of course. I think that, in a week or 10 days at most, I can go back to my routine."

A few more days passed, and she called again.

"I'll be there tomorrow," I reported happily.

"Oh, thank goodness!"

After I hung up, I stood there wondering what to think. Was it possible that at the age of 72, I was flirting over the phone? And with a 21-year-old?!

CHAPTER XV

Laura and the autumn

On my return to Maués, I went straight from the airport to Zanoni Magaldi's house to catch up on the news. Together, we visited his farm and then went next door to mine. We could feel rightfully proud. In a few more years, it would be truly viable to distill rosewood oil from leaves and branches alone.

Laura was late getting home that evening, and when she hopped off her bike, I saw she was loaded down with supermarket bags.

"We're going to celebrate tonight," she said. "I'm so happy you're back. I even bought a bottle of wine."

"I'm happy to be back too. Pity I can't have any wine. My liver needs TLC since my malaria."

Laura laughed. "But I can have some! I'll fix dinner."

We stayed up talking well into the night and went to bed late.

I was lying in the dark, pondering my peculiar situation, when the door opened and Laura entered in silence, visibly tense. She lay down next to me and embraced me in a way that left no room for doubt.

"I'm sorry. I've gotten used to sleeping here. Besides, I'm tired of being alone." And so what never should have happened did.

I never could have imagined that I'd experience something like this at my age. I suddenly felt strong and glad to be alive. During the first months of my relationship with Laura, I didn't realize – better put, I didn't want to realize – that my happiness wouldn't last long. I just wanted to live without thinking about the future, savoring every moment and every day to the utmost.

As time went on, I started feeling guilty. I was interfering with Laura's life, preventing her from finding someone with whom she could have children and a longer, less complicated relationship. As happy as she might have been at that moment, in a few years I would be a worn-out old man and she'd be my nurse. I was being selfish and unintentionally hurting someone very dear to me. I felt I had to break it off as soon as possible, regardless of how unhappy we would be at first.

Three months after my return to Maués, I was still there, with no talk of going home to Manaus. At that point, everybody knew about my affair with a girl of 20. My chess and tennis buddies must have taken great delight in discussing the size of the horns that would crown my head in a few years. Much more serious a matter was the question of Daniel and Sara and the whole family's potential reaction. Something had to be done.

I think that up until then, Laura had no idea of this inner conflict of mine. It was so moving to see the joy on her face. During one interlude of powerful intimacy and complicity, she whispered in my ear, "I want to have your baby."

I didn't say anything right then. But I felt it was my duty to explain to her that I didn't want any more children, for obvious reasons. It would be irresponsible on my part. At my age, I wouldn't be a good father, I wouldn't be able to raise a child properly, my family wasn't going to take to the idea at all, and, on top of that, it wouldn't be good for Laura. There was no lack of reasons. My observations set off our first and last fight.

"Don't worry, I'll know how to take care of my baby!" was Laura's offended retort.

"Don't talk foolish," I said, alarmed.

Even after this quarrel, which erased any doubts about how urgently I had to make a decision, I kept putting things off. Then, in September 1993, I received the sad news of my brother's untimely death. He had suffered a massive stroke, which in turn had caused a car accident. I was devastated – both sad and worried. "Something like this might happen to me," I told myself in my grief. Where would that leave Laura? And if she really got pregnant? I couldn't wait any longer. Laura's life was more important than my whims and desires.

As always, when I have a serious problem, I asked my late friend Salvator to help me; he's always with me. But this time, he was oddly silent. I talked the problem over with Magaldi, and he agreed that the situation couldn't go on. It was only then that I gathered up my courage and spoke to Laura. The conversation was much more difficult than I could have imagined. I repeated all of my arguments. I asked her to give me some time. I said I was going to Israel to offer my family my support. I told her she could stay on the farm as long as she wanted. And when I returned from Israel, we'd talk again. She cried, and I wanted so badly to take it all back, but I managed to stand firm. And so, rather hurriedly, I put an end to a fairy tale that could never have a happy ending.

Wishing I could just forget it all, I traveled to Israel to visit Ester, my brother's widow, and Dov, his son, with whom I'd never had much contact. Ester was a rather successful artist. She still lived on the kibbutz, where she was much loved and had no plans to leave. Dov was an engineering student in Jerusalem, not far from there. Life went on for them as always, even without David, and that made me think that we simply don't make any difference in this world.

I couldn't get Laura out of my head, and in my impatience, I cut short my stay in Israel and headed on to Bulgaria. I spent just a few days in Sofia, where I made a deal with a gypsy gentleman, who was always hanging around the cemetery gate, to take care of my parents' and grandparents' burial plots. I visited Salvator's grave too. I decided to go home via Vienna, as Max Haim had fallen ill with serious respiratory problems. We had a long talk at the hospital there, and I told him of my love story with Laura.

Max thought it over a little and then, wheezing hard, grew restless in his bed. "I remember her from the time we stayed in Maués. She was always helping her parents. She was a very pretty, polite teenager – looked exotic with black hair and a dark complexion. I've never forgotten her."

"Now she's a beautiful woman. I think she's a lot of sand for this old truck," I said, trying to make light. "I never should have let things get this far…"

"Licco, my friend, you're throwing your good fortune away! You've got it all wrong. Don't think about anyone else, just about you and this young woman. Go back to her and be happy as long as you can," Max reproached me. "Two thousand years ago, the Roman poet Horatio taught us how important it is to grab the present – his famous *carpe diem* – in recognition of how short life is – *memento mori*. From what I understand, you've still got some assets; leave them to her and don't worry. The holy books tell us that virtuous women know how to conduct themselves with dignity. Get going, fellow! We've only got one life to live."

I think that's what I wanted to hear. I headed back to Brazil the next day, and when I arrived in Manaus, I simply changed planes and continued on to Maués. At the farm, I found the house locked. The caretaker told me that Laura had traveled without saying where she was going or when she would return. In distress, I went into Maués to look for her. I hired a detective in Manaus and another one in Rio de Janeiro – her favorite city – but I never saw her again.

A little while later, I received news from Nissim Michael that my friend Max Haim had passed away. "I got there in time for his funeral," Nissim wrote. "As you know, his whole family was wiped out in a concentration camp, and he didn't have any close relatives. Nor did he ever marry or have children. In a way, Maria Luiza and I were his family in recent years. He'd visit us in Madrid, and we'd visit him in Vienna. That's why my presence was so important," he explained.

It wasn't easy to absorb yet another blow, and I told myself, "My good fortune – the good fortune Max talked about the last time we were together – has left me for good."

* * * * *

But the world kept right on turning. Flying in the face of Fukuyama's "End of History" theory, many things have happened since then. In Israel, a crazy extremist killed Yitzhak Rabin and thwarted peace negotiations in the Middle East. Without Rabin, Israel has not had a leader with enough authority to grant and receive concessions, and peace has seemed ever more distant. Six years after that, when boredom ruled supreme in the realm of History, the September 11 attacks occurred, providing the impetus for further conflicts. Ignoring the lessons of Vietnam, the U.S. got involved in not just one but two wars, with all their disastrous consequences. If you want to spend a lot of money, the wise men say, the most pleasurable way is to spend it on women, the most entertaining way is to spend it on gambling, and the most efficient, hands down, is to spend it making war. Nobody can dissuade me from the idea that the economic crisis afflicting the world since 2008 has a lot to do with the trillions of dollars wasted in the wars in Iraq and Afghanistan.

Meanwhile, Eastern European nations had started down the road to economic recovery following the collapse of the Berlin Wall, but they got stuck halfway there, far from prosperity. Given Bulgaria's own burdensome legacy and longstanding vices, it will be some time before the charming corner of Europe where I was born and spent the bulk of my youth becomes a just and thriving country, one that offers a quality place to live. This day has drawn much nearer, but for several generations, it will come too late to enjoy.

As old as I am, I still keep up with politics, economics, and culture in Brazil. Over the last 16 years, the nation's economy has improved markedly, especially in its victory over inflation. Its democratic institutions have also solidified and gained muscle. Yet growth remains pitiful, especially because the government interferes too much in the economy. Life in a globalized world seems more and more like a Formula 1 race, and right now our Ferrari isn't very competitive.

The big surprise in more recent years was the election of Dilma Rousseff, a woman and one with a Bulgarian heritage. Berta would have been doubly happy. Times are changing faster than we could have imagined, and driven, determined women are taking their rightful places. I'm rooting for Dilma to step out of her predecessor's shadow and enforce the fiscal, political, administrative, and social reforms that our country so badly needs. The phase of demagogic government handouts, sky-high taxes, and a government so heavy that we can't bear its weight is fading fast, and Dilma will have to foster the productivity, rationality, and meritocracy that are sorely missing.

After Laura left, I nearly gave up on the farm. I never went back, and my investments in the rosewood trees dwindled. My neighbor, Zanoni, managed to raise many more trees than I did. I almost got back into it in 2010, when rosewood was declared a protected species under CITES, an international agreement to guarantee the preservation of flora and fauna. I celebrated the decision, because I believed the sustainability model would receive incentive at last, with trees being planted so that oil could be harvested from their leaves and branches. But because of bloated bureaucracy, it soon became clear that the market could not guarantee an adequate supply. Brokenhearted, I watched the perfume and cosmetics industry eliminate rosewood oil from its formulas. I was sad but also disgusted, because if proper advantage had been taken of these plantings, we could have preserved the species while exploiting its tremendous economic potential. It would have been an incredible incentive for planting more. The myopic ecologists failed to understand that poverty and the absence of economic activity are the environment's worst enemies.

Looking back and taking stock, things haven't gone poorly for me, but I can't deny that I'm losing my zest for life as time goes by. At my age, we say goodbye to something every day: quality of life, someone we know and maybe love... In point of fact, now it's just Nissim in Madrid and me in Manaus. Since losing Maria Luiza, he's grown steadily sadder and more depressed. We exchange emails every now and again, and to my great surprise, I've discovered that as he nears the end, he's embraced the religion he abandoned so many years ago.

My friends and colleagues from over the years – from work, tennis, and chess – have slowly disappeared, and, despite the attention of my family, I'm feeling lonelier and lonelier.

ILKO MINEV

I try to keep busy with my books and the infinite music on this iPod that my children gave me (it's not so easy to figure out). They often give me these newfangled gadgets. They've also given me some prints by Romero Britto, a big name in Brazilian painting. I'm fascinated with his bright, almost gaudy colors, which echo our country's joyful soul.

CHAPTER XVI

A surprise called Rebeca

I was immersed in my loneliness when an unexpected event shook my life and renewed my zest for life. I was at home sitting on my favorite patio, catching a cool breeze, with my old German shepherd, Quilate, lying at my side, when I heard the doorbell. Terezinha and Quilate went to answer it. Soon, (comma) I saw a tall, bald gentleman come in; he had the air of retired military about him. I figured he must be from the interior.

Terezinha told me, "Mr. Hazan, this is Antenor from Tefé. He insists on talking to you alone." Then, she left us. Wordlessly, Antenor opened a manila folder, took out some pictures, and handed them to me. I looked at them without understanding, and without any real interest. Then, I felt a knife strike my heart. They were photos of Laura, some from many years before, others more recent, almost all of them featuring Antenor and a young girl as well. Mixed in, I spotted a picture of myself from 40 years earlier.

"Do you know this person?" Antenor asked.

"I do," I replied in a gravelly voice. "Where is she?"

"She was my wife for almost 20 years. She passed away last month. There was an outbreak of hemorrhagic dengue fever in Tefé, and she was one of the first to come down with it. It was the third time for her in two years, and she didn't make it," he said, bowing his head. "Before she passed away, she asked me to get in touch with you if anything happened to her. We've got a daughter, Rebeca." His voice choked up, and his words came hard. I could barely comprehend what was happening.

"Rebeca is my daughter, but the truth is, you're her biological father."

I was stunned. For a moment, I wondered whether the man was there to extort money from me. "No. No, this isn't about blackmail," I thought. He seemed to be a decent fellow. Anyway, nobody in the world could pretend that well. Antenor was close to tears. I asked him to tell me the whole story.

"I met Laura at a school in Maués. It was November 1992 – 18 years ago – and I was spending some time in town. I was taken by her as soon as we met. She was a great teacher – not to mention very pretty. I tried to get to know her, and it wasn't long before I realized she was sad, real lonely – and worried about something. It was easy to make friends with her since I'm a teacher too, and we had lots in common. It took her a while to open up to me, but at the end of the school year, in early December, when I was getting ready to travel to Belém, she got ahold of me and asked if she could go along. She wanted to leave Maués any way she could, and I reckoned it was about a broken heart or something like that," Antenor explained. "She gradually began to trust me. And then one day in Belém, she broke down crying and told me she was pregnant. At that point, I was head over heels, so I told her I loved her and wanted to marry her anyway and I'd raise the child as my own. We were married in March, but I have to confess that it was a real long time before she got over it and learned to love me." The teacher lowered his head again. "I think it only happened after Rebeca's birth, which was a really tough one. Both Laura and the baby almost died, but with the grace of God, they pulled through. We spent two years in Belém, then moved to Santarém. We eventually settled in Tefé, where we got good teaching jobs. That's where Laura is buried and where Rebeca and I still live."

He went on to tell me that Rebeca was 17, had already taken her college entrance exams, and had been accepted by the Federal University of Amazonas, where she was going to major in Portuguese language and literature. She'd always known that Antenor wasn't her biological father, and sometimes she'd ask who he was, but he and Laura preferred not to touch the subject.

"Laura never hid the father's identity from me, and I knew she never completely lost interest in you. Somehow she managed to keep up with news about you."

"Why didn't you and she ever contact me, Antenor?"

"Laura didn't want to, not at all. Me, even less. I think in a way, even at a distance, she continued to admire you. It never bothered me much. I almost never got jealous. Because she always made it clear that I was the man of her life," Antenor replied in a proud voice. And I was the one who felt jealous. "A little before she died, she asked me to talk to you and tell you the truth, if anything happened to her. She wanted you to have the chance to meet your...our daughter."

"Where is she? Of course I want to meet her!"

"She's at our hotel, but I could come back with her this afternoon. There's just one other thing. No matter what happens, she's still going to be my daughter." Those were Antenor's final words.

I felt a deep respect for the man. He was doing something extraordinary, and I knew that each word cost him dearly. I also knew he was telling the truth. And I could hardly wait to meet my daughter. It did occur to me that it wouldn't be easy to break the news to Daniel and Sara – that they'd just gained a sister, much younger than their own children.

I was very nervous when I met Rebeca that same afternoon. It took just one glance, and I knew she was Laura's daughter. But there was something else familiar about her that I couldn't put my finger on.

Rebeca wasn't very comfortable either. She kept squeezing her hands together, and I could tell she was examining me. Our conversation was strained, interspersed with small talk. Finally she said, "Mr. Hazan, maybe you can explain why my name is Rebeca."

It immediately hit me what was so painfully familiar about the young girl: her face bore the same expression as my father's, which had also been my brother David's trademark. There would be no need for any paternity test. She was my daughter.

"Rebeca? My dear, Rebeca was my mother's name."

I couldn't hold back the tears, and I felt nearly as drained as I had when I'd suffered from malaria. The ice between us broke, and both Antenor and Rebeca rushed to my side to help me. It was a struggle for me to pull myself together, and I saw that Rebeca's eyes were filled with tears too.

"When were you born?"

"On May 3, 1993."

"So when Laura and I separated, in early November, she knew she was pregnant," I thought. Saddened and aggrieved by yet another overwhelming piece of news, I remained silent in my pain.

* * * * *

Indeed, it wasn't easy telling Daniel and Sara the story. They were quite surprised, as to be expected. Perhaps because Sara is a judge and has had experience with so many different cases, she came around and accepted the news more readily. It took Daniel longer, and he insisted on a DNA test. Everyone thought it was odd that this story had not been revealed only now, when Rebeca was already an adult.

I found it interesting how quickly my grandchildren accepted the news, even cracking some harmless jokes. We had a big Shabbat dinner at Sara's house, where I introduced Rebeca to the whole family. I'm amazed at how younger generations are more tolerant about this type of thing. Although Rebeca is Catholic and my entire family is Jewish, to my delight, everyone got along well. A sign of the times.

A little while later, Daniel called me up and said, "Dad, there's no need for the test. She looks a lot like you. It's up to you."

In any case, I made it a point to have the test to avoid any problems down the road. Rebeca was still officially Antenor's daughter, but now she was part of our family too. And so we found a Solomonic solution, one that pleased all sides.

Less than a month later, Rebeca accepted my invitation and moved into my house in downtown Manaus. It's closer to the university, which would be good for her. At the same time, she would be good company for me, just as her mother had been 20 years earlier.

That's when I realized that my long and winding road was a story that deserved to be told to my children, Daniel, Sara, and Rebeca; to my four grandchildren, Berta, Samuel, Ilana, and Eli; to my six great-grandchildren; and to all those who will come after them. The family that Berta and I started with so much love years ago in Istanbul had thrived and multiplied.

It took me half a year to write this account of mine.

I've remembered so many things that I thought I'd forgotten forever, things that often moved me deeply. I've tried to tell my story simply and unpretentiously, recognizing myself as no more than a common man who happened to be an active participant in these events. This is why the act of writing has given me so much pleasure.

There's only one detail left: bidding Maués farewell. Daniel and Sara are against this urge of mine, and they want me to wait until one of them can go with me, but I don't have that much time. I again recall my friend Salvator, who once remarked between one bout of fever and another at the labor camp, "Licco my friend, if I could go back and live my short life over, I'd admire a lot more sunsets and sunrises, I'd enjoy the good things in life much more, and I'd do more *mitzvot*. But I'd also get up to a lot more mischief!"

That's it exactly. I know what has to be done. One last bit of mischief. Rebi *Shimon bar Yochai*, help me reach Maués!

Here ends my story. *Quod scripsi, scripsi*. What I have written, I have written.

EPILOGUE

The two envelopes

The phone rings in the middle of the night, and Rachel answers it. A sleeping Daniel hears his wife's frantic voice somewhere off in the distance. AEs he wakes up, he realizes something odd is going on. Rachel nudges him and says in a rush, "Daniel, your dad went out early yesterday morning and hasn't come back yet. Terezinha is worried to death."

"How'd he go out? He doesn't drive anymore. I can't believe he didn't leave a note saying where he was going and when he'd get back. I guess we'd better find out what's going on."

Daniel throws on some clothes and hurries over to his father's house, where Sara and Rebeca are waiting for him. They form a veritable war council. Terezinha tells them that Licco left with Joaquim, a cabbie who drives the old man around a lot, and that he took Quilate along.

Daniel tries to get through to Joaquim on the cabbie's cell phone, but all he gets is a message saying the phone is outside the service area. He calls the driver's house, and his wife tells him Joaquim has gone to spend a few days in the country.

"At least they're together and Quilate is there to keep them company," Daniel thinks aloud.

Sara bursts out in a laugh. "I bet he's in Maués. Let's call Magaldi."

"Of course. He went to say his goodbyes – he's always been crazy about that place." Daniel understands what's going on now. "And he took Quilate along… The dog was born there, and he's as old as the hills too."

They call Zanoni Magaldi's cell, and he answers on the first ring. Magaldi doesn't say anything, just hands the phone to someone else. When Daniel recognizes the familiar voice on the other end of the line, he can't help but blow up. "Dad, you can't do stuff like this! You gave us all heart attacks!"

"I can't talk right now. We're getting on the boat to Itacoatiara. I'll be back in Manaus early tomorrow morning. Don't worry about me. I'm very, very happy." He hangs up.

"Sara and Rebeca, I'm going to drive out to Itacoatiara and wait there for the old coot," Daniel says. "Want to come along? It's a three-hour ride."

Those three hours seem to take forever. When they finally meet Licco at the port in Itacoatiara, he's burning up with fever and can barely move.

"He was agitated last night, kept saying over and over again how happy he was. Managed to take a walk in the rosewood trees at the farm," Joaquim reports. "Then, he sat on the terrace for a long time, staring out at the river and beach. Didn't want anybody bothering him. I watched him from a ways away, and he looked like he was carrying on a conversation with someone invisible. Later on, back inside, he opened a bottle of wine, had a sip, gave the rest to the caretaker. Then, he flipped through some old books on the shelf, muttered something about lost flowers, and went to bed," the cabbie says. "Quilate seemed agitated too. He and that other German shepherd on the farm – Quilate's brother – they weren't getting along at first, but then they must've recognized each other, 'cause they made friends and went off to play in the river. Caretaker said they're both descendants of Quixote, that fine German shepherd Mrs. Hazan brought to the farm years ago."

They hang on the words of Joaquim, the faithful cabbie who'd driven Licco there.

"No trouble overnight. Zanoni came to pick us up in the morning. We went to see the rosewood grove and then started back. That's when you folks called. Old man said goodbye to Zanoni, we got in the boat, he snoozed a bit. When he woke up, he had a coughing fit, and that's when he started getting sick. His fever just kept on climbing and must be pretty high right now."

The fever doesn't come down even with the help of medication. The doctors announce that he has double pneumonia. It refuses to respond to treatment. Two days later, Licco passes away. His expression is one of peace. He even seems to have a little smile on his face.

While family and friends sit *abel* in mourning, long-toothed Quilate does nothing but lie next to Licco's favorite chair. He doesn't have the strength to get up or even eat.

"Quilate's near the end too," Daniel sadly notes. "He won't last long now. Every once in a while, he lets out a howl that breaks my heart. Dad was really his only true master."

"The last few months, Licco spent hours and hours on the computer, writing away," Rebeca remarks. "I took him to the Berimex office last week 'cause he wanted to print out a really long file. I remember I teased him, asking if he'd written a dissertation. He laughed and said he had in a way. I saw him put the printout in the safe."

Daniel, Sara, and Rebeca go into the small office and

open the safe, an old relic from the days of the Brits. They find two envelopes inside, one thin and the other quite fat.

Daniel opens the smaller of the two and reads it aloud.

Dear loved ones,

When you read this letter, I will no longer be with you. I can't say it enough: strength comes through union, and that's why I want you all to stay united forever. Although Rebeca isn't officially a Hazan, she's my daughter, and she's part of our family. I hope my children, grandchildren, and great-grandchildren will live together in peace and harmony and will help one other, come what may. Remember that your cousins Oleg and Dov and their descendants are also part of our clan.

I'm not one for big shows of bereavement, so it's enough that you remember my nahala *and say* Kaddish *once a year.* Dayenu!

All of the family business is already in Daniel's and Sara's names, so I want to leave the house to Rebeca. I've got two big CDs at the bank, both from the recent sale of the weekend homes that Berta and I bought in the 1970s – their values skyrocketed. I'd like the larger of these to be used for the education of Rebeca, my grandchildren, and my great-grandchildren at the finest universities.

I'd like the smaller one to go 100 percent to Rebeca. I'd like the rosewood farm in Maués to be divided equally between Daniel, Sara, and Rebeca. I still hold out hope that producing this oil will one day be good business for the Amazon again. Common sense shall prevail.

I wish you all the very best! Have some patience, and read the story of my life (in the other envelope) with care. I hope it will be helpful to you as you face the difficult task of tackling whatever challenges the future may bring

– do it enthusiastically, responsibly, and wisely.

May the blessings of God rest upon you always! Your father, grandfather, and great-grandfather loves you very much.

Licco Hazan

Sara opens the second envelope, takes out a sheaf of crudely bound pages, and begins to read:

In the autumn of my life, before illness or senility silence me...

GLOSSARY

abel: the first days of mourning after a death (also known as shiva)

aliyah: a Jew's immigration to Israel

Aljama: a term once used in Portugal for a Jewish neighborhood

Avenue of the Righteous among Nations: a pathway at the Yad Vashem memorial where trees are planted for each person who helped save lives during World War II (e.g., Oskar Schindler)

aviador houses: companies that formerly sold on credit in the interior of the Amazon

bar mitzvah: Jewish ceremony celebrating the coming of age of a young boy at age 13

brit milah: Jewish circumcision ceremony

caboclo (cabocla – fem.): 1. an individual of mixed white and indigenous ethnicity; 2. a native of the Amazonian interior

Capablanca: Cuban chess player and world champion for almost a decade in the 1920s

chazan: a cantor at a synagogue

dayenu: a Hebrew expression that means for me, that will suffice

Diaspora: the scattering of the Jewish people to all corners of the earth

Essel Abraham: synagogue in Belém; literally, the inn of Abraham

FOB (Free On Board): is a term in United States and international commercial law specifying at what point the seller transfers ownership of the goods to the buyer.

Hanukkah: Jewish Festival of Lights

Hekhal: Ladino term for the ark where the sacred Torah scrolls are kept

Hochdeutsch: high German; standard literary German once spoken only by the elite

IBAMA: Brazilian Institute for the Environment and Renewable Natural Resources, Brazil's environmental protection agency

INPA: National Institute for Research in the Amazon

Juderia: a term once used in Spain for a Jewish neighborhood

Kaddish: the Jewish prayer for the dead

kibbutz: an Israeli cooperative farm, where everything is shared according to the needs of each, in keeping with socialist principles

Kol Nidre: one of the main prayers of Yom Kippur (defined below)

Ladino: language used by Sephardic Jews

mazel tov: Yiddish expression meaning congratulations or good luck

minyan: quorum of 10 Jewish men, often required to perform prayer

mitzvah (singular of mitzvot): Hebrew for good deed

nahala (singular of nahalot): Hebrew for the anniversary of someone's death

Passover (also known as Pesach): Jewish celebration of the Hebrews' escape from slavery in Egypt around 1280 B.C.

patriarch: leader of the Eastern Orthodox Church

Reichstag: the parliament of Nazi Germany

river-mining dredge: a dredge that turns over the bottom of a river and removes gravel and sand through a 10-inch suction pump, leaving a crater nearly 100 feet deep; the dredged material is processed and the gold extracted on the vessel itself, which is also where the prospectors live

Rosh Hashana: Jewish New Year

Sephardic: Jew from the Iberian Peninsula; Hebrew for Iberian Peninsula

Sha'ar Hashomayim: Synagogue in Belem, which means gate of heaven in Hebrew

Shabbat: the Jewish Sabbath, the day of rest

shalom: Hebrew for peace

sheliah: officiant, cantor, and reader of Jewish holy scripture

Shimon bar Yochai (also known as Simeon bar Yochai): a first-century sage, believed by many Jews to be a miracle worker

shofar: ram's horn trumpet used in Jewish ceremonies

Sukkot: the Jewish Feast of Tabernacles, celebrated in early autumn

Sveta Nedelya Cathedral: an Eastern Orthodox cathedral in Sofia

Torah: the holy book of Judaism

Yiddish: the language used by Jews in Central and Eastern Europe

Yom Kippur: the Jewish Day of Atonement, which falls 10 days after Rosh Hashana